MALADY

A NECROSIS OF THE MIND DUET

TRISHA WOLFE

LOCK KEY PRESS

"It is true, we shall be monsters, cut off from all the world; but on that account we shall be more attached to one another."

— Mary Shelley, Frankenstein

HUNT

BLAKELY

*D*evil's Peak looks different in the daylight.

The dark canopy of trees I've only glimpsed at night, that felt so nefarious with their gnarled limbs vying to steal the stars from my view, catches the sun's rays to send glittering shards across the pine straw-covered ground.

The forest is in full bloom. Bright greens and oranges mingle with the heavily wooded backdrop of brown, like a Bob Ross painting with his happy little trees. It's a sight right out of Vanessa's pastel drawing room. The scent of the forest even smells pastel.

Before me, the narrow river is gray, the river stones tinting the clear water as the stream moves at a peaceful pace, the current leisure and serene. A tranquil atmosphere that is in direct contrast to the horrors of my nightmares.

Alex belonged to the night.

He was a creature of the moon and shadows.

He was Devil's Peak, and he couldn't have chosen a better location for his sinister research lab, where he tortured his victims in the name of science. Oh, he believed—somewhere in his delusional brain—that he was fighting a just cause, but it was ultimately a selfish cause. One that gave his deceased, psychotic twin sister a chance to redeem her tarnished reputation.

She made her choices, though. And Alex made his.

For her crimes against her patients, Alex's sister was murdered by a psychopathic vigilante serial killer. Instead of mourning her loss, accepting who his sister was, Alex picked up her torch and conducted cruel experiments on people in order to try to cure psychopathy.

We're all products of our choices. Somehow mine led me to this place, and I've been trying to escape it ever since. My mind is trapped here, no matter how far away I run.

I pull my hoodie close and cross my arms over my chest as I stroll toward the river. I'm cautious of the riverbank, where the graveyard of Alex's "expired" subjects lie. I discovered the partially dissolved remains the day I escaped, when I fell into the bones. I still have the scar on my palm.

A bird chirps in the distance, and I glance out over the mountain peaks, relieved my attention has been diverted. Only now, as my gaze tracks the bird's path, the distinct splash of the waterfall pricks my ears. Chill bumps ripple across my skin.

An alarming flutter attacks my chest. I cover the ache with my hand, palm pressed to my breastplate. I despise that I have absolutely no control over these traitorous feelings—that just the thought of seeing the waterfall cascading down the cliff causes the beat of my heart to quicken.

My mind summons the sensation of the cool, rough stone under my back. I can feel the icy water biting into my skin and his heated touch chasing away the chill to ignite me from the inside as his hands discover my body. And his kiss…

My chest burns as I remember the feel of his lips, how he deepened the kiss, our breath exchanged and stolen, as I became lost to him.

I fasten my eyes shut, effectively shutting down the memory.

With gathered strength, I turn my back to the river and force my booted feet onto the path. I thought I needed to face that place, to see it again and discover if it evoked the same emotions I felt that night. But I haven't even glimpsed the waterfall and I'm already shaken.

I loathe this weakness.

Keeping my gaze cast on the worn trail, I avoid looking at the cabin until I reach the gate. I pull in a fortifying breath and flip the latch. The gate pushes open with a shrill squeak.

The sight halts my steps. The charred husk of the house stands in a dilapidated state of ruin where Alex's little cabin once existed. The roof has fallen in. Blackened wood beams jut upward from the ground, bare and naked, the walls piled in heaps atop the scorched earth.

As I move closer, I notice where the trees nearest the fire were seared, but they must have been far enough from the flames to only sustain minimal damage. This whole forest should have burned. On instinct, I gravitate toward the basement door. It's still open from where I escaped, the fire having grazed one of the doors.

A panicked beat flips my heart as I stare down into the dark vault where Alex kept me for almost a month. The smell of acrid fire and wet soot wafts up from the belly of the pit. I won't go down there, not if I can help it. I look away and continue through the wreckage, knowing why I'm here, what I'm searching for, and somehow still terrified to discover it.

Three weeks ago, I felt the telltale prickle on the

back of my neck, the signature predator and prey internal alarm that I was being watched.

Paranoia, maybe.

A remnant of the weeks I spent as a captive to a mad scientist, absolutely.

Then the first body was discovered, and I could no longer discount my suspicions.

One of my revenge targets dying doesn't set off an alarm—but two killed in a suspected "mugging" and stabbed numerous times...

That's more than suspicious.

That's a cry from the grave.

I'll never sleep again if I don't see the proof with my own eyes. I'll never believe he's not just around a corner, watching. Waiting.

And I refuse to live in fear.

If Alex burned alive in this fire, I want to see the bones.

I want them to crumble to ash beneath my boots as I walk over them.

Hate is a new emotion for me. I was accustomed to indifference, and this dark, consuming feeling eating me from the inside needs an outlet. Even as I studied human emotion my whole life in order to mimic it, I never realized that it's not just one emotion being felt at a time.

Every emotion has a web of underlying sub-feelings that battle for dominance.

It's complicated and exhausting. No wonder why most people confuse me; they have absolutely no fucking idea what they're feeling most days.

I shake off tiring thoughts and continue to search the cabin. To get here, I employed the skills I once used to deliver retribution for my clients. I tracked down the tow truck driver. He still had Alex's little two-door truck on his lot. I rented a car, drove straight there, and dug out the registration from the glovebox. The address was listed in the nearest town—so that gave me a starting point.

Fleeing a house engulfed in flames with an unhinged madman who had just demolished his disturbing room of clocks makes one forget important details, like how the hell I got away. I remember escaping the cabin. Driving the truck through the woods. Making it to a rest stop where I called a tow truck service. But the finer details are a haze blotted out by adrenaline and heightened emotion.

But once I was heading in the right direction, the scenery started to become familiar, and I knew I was on the right path. As if some force was drawing me back to Devil's Peak.

I trace my fingers along a charred beam. The seared, blackened wood is coarse and abrasive. I used to be like this wood, hardened, damaged but resilient. I used to face every intense situation with a calm and unaffected demeanor, and I would have handled that night differently had it not been for the emotions Alex cursed me with.

My fingers curl around a splinter of the beam. The wood breaks away, and I crumble it in my palm before letting the sooty ash fall to the earth.

I stare at the black smudges, the way the grime lines the grooves of my palm.

I've made a mess.

As I wipe my hand on my jean-clad thigh, I walk toward the center of the house, to where I think Alex's dark room was located. Where I last saw him.

My heart beats faster. I am absolutely terrified to find Alex's remains—but I'm even more terrified *not* to find him.

I haven't slept a full night since I escaped. Sleep deprivation can play havoc on the mind, can make you question your reality. There's a terrible fear creeping within me that, somehow, I'm responsible for what's happened to my targets. Or worse…

Alex fucked with my brain—I've done things, horrific things—and I'm not the same person. What am I capable of? Serial murder? Could I kill a person and block it from my mind like it's just another one of my nightmares?

No—I'm not going there. Not yet.

The nightmares will stop once I literally bury the past. Despite all I've suffered, despite my darkest fears, Alex needs to be lain to rest.

The deeper I head into the ruin, the more my unease grows. My head pulses, and I touch my temple, noting the rough feel of scar tissue. The blistered flesh from the electrodes of Alex's crude electroshock machine. It's as if the closer I get to finding him, the more alive the pain becomes.

Only, after searching for over an hour, I don't find him. No charred flesh. No bones.

No body.

There are no remains other than this dead house.

A sense of dread coils around my spine, my muscles tight and skin hot.

I could rummage below the wreckage. I could dig beneath this dilapidated heap and search the forest beyond. But in the end, I'd just be even more soot-covered and filthy, because my nightmares are real. The dread of being watched isn't some lingering victim bullshit.

The deranged scientist isn't here.

I follow the skeletal remains of the house like a blueprint, trekking through a narrow space that leads to the backside where I stop and stare out into the forest.

Where the brush along the tree line has been cleared from the fire, a small wooden shack appears. Trepidation claws at my nerves as I encroach on the structure. I can make out tread marks in the rain-sodden earth.

The shack doors are open, revealing an empty

inside, but the evidence on the ground exposes what was once stored here. Alex kept a second vehicle on site. And by the look of the tire marks, it was a motorcycle.

"Son-of-a-bitch."

A bird twitters in the tree above and I startle, hand pressed to my chest. I whirl around, my gaze darting from the cabin to the woods. Anger chews through the anxiety. I lower my hand and ball my fingers into a tight fist.

There's one thing I've learned in my short time with these infuriating emotions, and that's the only way to control them is to focus all my uncertainty and fear—drill it down into a sharp point—and channel it into fury.

Then I direct all the fury toward Alex.

I pull my phone out and check the time, making sure I have enough to get to the airport. Just the quick action of looking at the time has my pulse spiking. I'll never view clocks the same again.

Alex ruined a lot of things for me. Most notably, the career I loved.

I haven't taken a new revenge job since Lenora Daverns. She was my last client. She severed all ties to me, and I deleted all connection to her after the way that job ended. *Ended* is a poor descriptor for the way I murdered her husband.

To make absolutely sure our arrangement remained a secret, I dug out my black notebook full of clients and their secrets—a contingency I always made sure to have in place should a job go badly—and hinted (okay, full on blackmailed) to Lenora that, should the authorities discover our arrangement, her private adoption would be made public. However, Lenora had no plans to reveal our connection; she was glad Ericson was gone.

"He was a monster," she had said.

In the end, Lenora learned who her husband truly was. And in that regard, Ericson might have had it coming. Hell, the shady criminals he was tied to were probably planning to take him out at some point, and I undoubtedly did them and every female escort in the city a favor. But, brutally stabbing a man to death in an alleyway is an act not even I can live with.

If Lenora suspects me of Ericson's death, she hasn't breathed a word. I discovered the insurance policy paid out to her was quite considerable. Maybe that's why she's staying silent, or maybe it was my not-so-veiled threat. I should stop obsessing over it, but the constant fear and paranoia has churned itself into neurosis. There's still evidence, little pieces of metadata, that links us together. If anyone digs hard enough, it's not impossible to uncover.

I've never been on the wrong side of the law before, and I'm running out of time.

The only person I've confided in is Jeffery Lomax, a family law attorney who refers his irreconcilable clients to my business. Well, he used to, back when I was revenge for hire. After I retained Lomax as my counsel with a dollar so our conversation remains bound by privilege, I told him my story, to which he recommended a cutthroat criminal defense lawyer.

In all honesty, I'm surprised he didn't refer me to a shrink.

I have the card for one Josh Vanson in my billfold. I haven't placed any calls to Vanson. Not yet. As far as the official report and the information I've gleaned from the news, the police aren't looking at anyone in connection to Ericson.

But a man is dead.

By my hands.

Yes, Ericson was a sadistic rapist and possible murderer himself, but that doesn't exonerate me of my actions.

I'm not running.

I plan to turn myself in and face my consequences like a woman.

But not before I get *my* revenge.

Before I confess to any crime, I have to find Alex. He did this to me. He turned me into this weak and disgusting...whatever I've become. And he's going to undo it. He's going to reverse the damage he's done to my brain, uncross the wires that got crossed, or whatever the fucking hell he has to do to bring me back.

I won't make it even one day in prison like this. I'll

break. I'll decay. I'll wither into a carcass just like this house.

The old Blakely could handle prison. She was tough and indifferent, nothing would affect her. She could defend herself against prisoners and not get duped by sentiment.

I need her in order to survive.

With an angry huff, I tug the hoodie over my head and start in the direction I came. I've seen enough. Alex isn't here. He abandoned his project, then burned the whole maniacal experiment to the ground.

And now he's out there.

Ultimately, what boils my blood—even if I can't admit it aloud—is that he abandoned me.

He forced me to feel all these things...things I can't even explain...so much so that the sheer overwhelm exhausts me daily.

Then he just left me alone to deal with it all.

My pulse thuds heavily in my ears as I pass the open basement door. Memories of Alex—his masculine scent, his pale-blue eyes, his messy dark hair, those dimples when he smiled his boyish smile—become too much, and I slam the door closed with a resounding *bang*.

He ruined my well-constructed life, yes, but he also ruined other things, too.

Like sex.

Sex was always simple. Uncomplicated. Find a person I'm attracted to and satisfy the need. It was never any deeper than that. Never any messy feelings to muddle through. I had sex the way I lived my life: pleasure-focused. Driven by my desires.

Then one night under a waterfall with Alex changed everything.

An ache blooms in my chest, like a bruise that won't heal, the fiery pain becoming a familiar companion. Thoughts of that night assault me. Of Alex as he touched me in a way no other man had, of how I could *feel* his need for me, feel his emotions, feel an intense connection to him.

He told me he loved me.

"He's the enemy," I say under my breath, a reminder that I can't lose sight of what he did. He tortured me for almost a month. He altered the chemistry of my brain, for fuck's sake.

And yet, on the nights when it's the hardest to sleep, when the sickness pits out my stomach and I curl into myself and I can't decipher the difference between anger and heartache, I reach for his shirt. The one I keep tucked on the side of the bed, the one I grabbed when I raced out of the burning cabin.

The one that still carries his scent of sandalwood and aquatic cologne and some indefinable masculine fragrance that belonged only to Alex.

I wear his shirt and, on some subconscious level, the comfort that closeness brings is enough to chase back the darkness.

The acrid smell of fire coats my throat, making it raw. I swallow hard. As I find my way back onto the path, I notice a shiny glint up ahead near the gate. The sun catches on the gleaming object, and as I get closer, a shiver rocks me.

I kneel down and swipe the dirt away with a shaky hand to uncover the pewter cover of Alex's pocket watch.

My heart knocks violently against my rib cage as I unearth the watch. The glass face is missing, the glass shattered and left discarded in the dirt. The gears are crushed and the hands no longer tick.

A strange eeriness settles over me at the silence, the world suddenly too quiet, too still.

Alex destroyed his timepiece right before he smashed every clock in his twisted dark room and set fire to his cabin.

In doing so, he set me free. But really, he only locked me inside a different kind of cage.

I rub my thumb over the engraving, the one Alex's sister had inscribed, before I clean the dirt out the best I can. I stand and slip the watch into my pocket.

Time haunts me.

The internal ticking of Alex's clocks is the soundtrack to my nightmares.

I'll get out of here. And when I do, Alex, I will hunt you down. I will end you. Through the hollow expanse of time, my words echo around this place filled with death and despair to come back to me in severe clarity, a vow I swore to Alex.

I will find him.

I will have my revenge.

But first, there's someone I need to meet.

TARGET PRACTICE

ALEX

I have loved to the point of madness.

I never fully appreciated the meaning of Sagan's verse until I crossed paths with Blakely Vaughn.

She changed everything.

She changed me.

I'm no longer the same man, reformed on a molecular level.

Even my cells crave her, to be connected.

I find myself reciting the verse every time an image of her comes to me. The way her teeth sink into her bottom lip so teasingly. The way she crosses her long legs, knowing just how seductive she is. The way she stares straight through me with those bottomless, sea-green eyes, down to the rotten marrow in my bones.

I never felt more alive, more out of control, then when I was around her. Normally, that would terrify me. Loss of control goes against everything I stand for. But with her, it was easy to allow my primal, wild beast to revel in base pleasures.

She makes me weak, but also stronger than I've ever felt.

I trace my fingertips over the sketch of her face, infusing Sagan's words into my system the way she infuses my whole being.

She is maddeningly a part of me now.

Mind, body, soul. My obsession consumes me from the inside out. Like the Carrion beetle burrowing to feast on decay, my necrotic matter called to her, and she devoured my rotted humanity to resurrect a new man.

I wasn't strong enough for her then.

But I am now.

No matter what she professed at the river, I know the truth. She tried to deny what she felt—*truly* felt—when we made love under the fall.

But I felt her wilt in my arms. The strong, stubborn, unbreakable Blakely shattered beneath me. She broke against me as we came together, melding two souls into one. A sublime collision of lust and longing, and pure, unadulterated ecstasy.

Her emotions scared her. She'd never experienced

them before. I had never experienced anything like *her* before. We connected on a plane above morals and judgement, and that's what frightened her.

She's fallen in love with her villain.

The mad scientist she loathes. Her tormentor. The one she envisions when she smashes her fist into the punching bag, and the one she thinks about when she touches herself.

And, oh, she's so painfully beautiful in her torment, in her confliction, the denial that festers her once-impenetrable resolve. I've seen what's under that hard layer, and it's vulnerable and tender and starved.

And it's mine.

Using my thumb to smudge the shadowed contour along her jawline, I blow away the lead debris, mindful not to impact her lips. Captured in perfect lighting under an illuminated marquee sign, her lips are flawless. Her features divine.

A single moment stolen.

I give myself credit, I've been patient. I watched her the other night as she waited to cross the street. The whole city abuzz around her as she stood motionless. A lost soul amid a sea of strangers all bustling with energy. And Blakely, arms crossed around her trim waist, trying to disappear in the stream.

I've been watching for a while, monitoring her progress, cataloging her setbacks, waiting on the sidelines to intervene. Her life is very different now.

Blakely no longer lurks in the shadows targeting victims for other people's revenge. Like standing beneath that brilliant sign, she's been thrust into the light, forced to interact with the world.

Since I returned to the city, I've been studying her cautiously, warily, the way I should have done before. Instead, I jumped in on impulse, too excited by the prospect she held. The lure to be pulled in by her gravity too compelling.

No more rash decisions. I need verifiable proof the procedure worked, not my biased assertion of what I witnessed during our last moments together. That, and the fact when I was faced with my demons, I made the reprehensible decision to destroy my lab and all my work.

It takes time to rebuild. And to rebuild better. If I can prove the results, then there is no guilt, no reason to feel anything other than pride at my accomplishment.

So I destroyed the research lab at the cabin, all the evidence, thereby allowing Blakely to believe I was destroyed also.

How else would she have been able to return to her life?

Once I have concrete, factual findings, I will atone for my sins with her, but I have no plans of spending the remainder of my life in prison. And I won't let Blakely, either.

I admit, the second I realized the treatment was a

success, the scientist in me was tempted to go directly to her. Eager to run tests and compare data, to study and map her neural pathways like Theseus exploring the labyrinth.

But really, the truth is far more sinister.

I'm not the hero slaying a disease.

I'm the monster in the center of the maze.

The selfish, needy man in me just wants her. To see the look in her eyes when I appear in her life. Alive. With the realization that I've come back for her.

A fiery pang resonates in my chest as I play out that delightful reunion in my head, intoned with a thick layer of sarcasm. I'm a pathetic heathen, disgusted with the fear that holds me at bay from her. The crushing, debilitating fear of rejection that, when our moment comes, Blakely will never accept us.

Of course, I did abduct her. Torture her. Conduct mind-altering experiments on her.

But oh, Blakely, if you'd only understand what greatness we could achieve together.

She was never meant for a mediocre life. We can be so much more. A breakthrough of this significance… I haven't even stopped long enough to imagine all the possibilities.

First, however, we have to contend with her guilt. It's holding her back. I aimed to make her feel that guilt, now I want to abate it. Guilt over scum like Ericson is wasted effort. The desire to go to her thrums through me with vicious longing but, as Blakely is the first successful test subject, I need to take my time collecting data, observing her, analyzing every detail. I can't rush this process. Not this time.

I was impulsive and emotional when I determined the experiment a failure. I terminated the whole project in one extreme, explosive production. That's what our uncontrollable emotions will do if not contained. Make us set fire to our entire life in one moment of uncertainty.

As Blakely clearly demonstrated by sticking a blade into a man.

If I had any doubts before about her transformation, that one act removed all skepticism.

The purpose of my project was so brilliant in its simplicity. Alter the brain chemistry, alter the individual. Change the world.

A new world where psychopaths suffered empathy. Where they would grieve should they make others grieve. A punishment just for those who didn't fear the world's justice system—a system designed imperfectly to let those offenders free.

The page crumples in my fisted hand. I loosen my strained shoulders, releasing a leaden breath. I flex my wounded hand, feeling the tightness of the ruined flesh beneath the bandage, then smooth out the creases in the page over Blakely's face.

Pain is real. It grounds me in the present.

Since the conception of my project, I've been keeping track of time but ultimately losing touch with the world. The importance of the here and now. All the moments that make this intolerable life worth living.

I was clear in my directive. Sure of what I was and my purpose. I couldn't see beyond the next step of the project. I couldn't imagine a higher purpose. I was so consumed with the immediate result, it wasn't until I stood outside my cabin, watching the flames lick high into the night, that I realized how misguided I had been.

Blakely had been a siren sent to lure me and infect my brain.

Her rejection made me doubt myself in that one defining moment. More so, it made me question who I am as a scientist. I questioned my methods; I had remorse for my subjects. I nearly ended my life.

And *why*? For *what*? Guilt has no place within the scientific method. I've realized this now. Hell, no one posted missing persons' posters or funded websites to find those people. They were vagrants. Their lives wasted.

I gave their lives meaning.

Blakely accused me of having a god complex; she compared me to Dr. Frankenstein, and ultimately, that may be true. As a biomedical scientist, a certain level of god-like ego is necessary. After all, the curing of diseases is simply another form of creation. I take the abnormality and design a treatment, coding the building blocks of DNA to correct the defect.

With her, I gave life to the dead. I brought the dead parts of her to life. I brought her to the world of the feeling.

I am a god.

And she is my creation.

She is my beautiful monster.

How can I not love her? She harbors a piece of me. As Eve was created from Adam's rib, Blakely's mind was designed by my science—a piece of me so intimate, it's the very nature of my being.

I cannot exist without her.

Unlike Dr. Frankenstein, I won't abandon my creation.

For ours is a script torn right from the pages of a Shakespearean play. That's the misfortune. Where do we go, how do we end, when we were fated to be a tragedy?

I have to alter every facet, change all the components. I have to rewrite the whole script to give us a redemptive ending.

If I can master altering the very fabric of her neural pathways, then I can change our outcome.

I just need time.

The USB drive in my pocket is noticeable and distinctly different from the weight of the pocket watch I used to carry. But on that drive is the formula for the newest iteration of the compound, the one I administered to Blakely.

The cure to psychopathy.

The urge to check the time crawls under my skin like a burrowing deathwatch beetle. I can hear its warning screech. Anxiety festers at the edge of my mind.

She's late.

Something's wrong. I can feel it in my cells, the way I can sense a storm brewing as the barometric pressure falls with a charge in the air. The atmosphere is crackling.

Blakely does as she wants, goes where she wants, but she's never late for this particular activity. In her new and unsure state of being, this is the one pursuit she believes gives her control.

Under the marquee sign, the giant plate-glass window reads: Martial Arts Training.

I scratch at my arm, the itch digging in deep. The niggling desire to know the time winds around me like a tightened spring, the coil tension near snapping.

I dig out my phone from my back pocket and wince at the pain. The burned flesh of my hand is still tender and in the stages of healing. As I light the phone screen to display the time, instant relief fills me, like getting a hit of a favorite drug, my craving subdued.

That relief quickly dissipates as a severe realization sinks in. Blakely isn't coming. She's changed her routine. The possible reasons for her sudden departure in routine vary, but there's only one motive that has my heart rate climbing.

She knows I'm watching.

I quash the thought immediately. I'm careful. I'm *very* careful, and I've kept my distance. At no time during the past six weeks has there been any indication that she's aware of me. Yet here we are, and I can't quell the alarm firing through my body.

I pack away my journal and hike the green rucksack over one shoulder. A final glance at the doorway of the martial arts studio, then I set off down the sidewalk toward Tribeca.

Desperation tightens around my chest like a band, the pain acute and demanding. My skin feels clammy, my breathing labored, as I frustratedly drive my hand through my hair. Normally, I'd turn to my devices and applications to locate a subject, but my little monster is smart. Just so, so clever. She's been off the grid, limiting her Internet activity and using a burner phone with no Wi-Fi access. My senses are all I have to track her.

The city is muggy, stifling, as I weave through the teeming crosswalk. Even the air is dense and feels crowded as it presses against my skin. I reach the brownstone and unlock the front door of my new apartment, the one I secured a block away from Blakely's place. It wasn't an easy acquire; the landlord had to be persuaded. But with a hefty down payment and six-month's rent paid in advance, the overpriced closet is mine and in a prime location to keep watch over my subject.

I unload my pack at the entryway and, like every other time I've done so, seek the comfort of seeing Mary's face. There's no comfort, however. No framed photo of us when we were kids. None of her Renaissance paintings line my walls.

I had to leave my worldly belongings behind. A dead man doesn't return to clean out his apartment. And Blakely checked. Twice. As if needing confirmation that I was really gone, she went through my mail. She watched my loft, stalking my old haunt the way she used to stalk her targets.

With a resigned frown, I glance around the sparsely furnished studio. Eventually, the landlord of my old place will either auction off my possessions or toss them.

I stop in the kitchen to grab a water from the fridge. Door held open, I relish the cool refrigerated air as it blasts my slick skin, gaze landing on the top shelf with the five glass vials.

A *thump* snags my attention, and I hastily guzzle from a water bottle before I grab one of the vials and head into the bathroom.

Location wasn't the only reason why I chose this place. The converted studio next door was condemned due to a fire. Renovations stalled when the price of building materials went sky-high, leaving the place vacant. With the state of the economy, the project is likely to stay abandoned for the foreseeable future.

I slip the vial in my pocket before removing the bathroom mirror to expose the hole in the wall. Cut large enough to crawl through, I clear the opening and enter the dark apartment.

The air inside here is only marginally less humid than outside. The unit doesn't have power, so I had to utilize the electricity from mine. I drilled a small hole through the baseboard and wall to run two power cords, which feed power to the devices I consider more vital than air-conditioning.

The *thump* comes louder this time, and my phone buzzes in my back pocket with the alarm.

I turn off the reminder, then set my phone on the bare metal table. Construction debris and dust covers the unit. The wood floors have been pried up in areas. Cabinets ripped out. The walls have been stripped to reveal the original brick. It reminds me of Mary's cabin in a way, the age and history, the solid bones.

I take a syringe from the basket under the table. "The anesthesia wore off quicker than anticipated. I'll account for that from now on."

As I fill the syringe with the contents of the vial, the restrained man in the center of the room groans and wriggles against his bindings. I was able to secure an old gurney from a hospital's dumpsite, but unfortunately, I did have to break into my retirement fund to acquire all new computers and lab equipment.

The black market is where I earn a living these days, selling hacking software and cloning prototypes. I recall once telling Blakely I had no intention of doing so, but the ends justify the means. I need money—lots of it—to fund a new project.

Since time is of the essence, I forewent building another brain scanner and mapping device, and instead purchased the instruments direct from a Korean lab.

It's risky, conducting the experiment in the city. I thought I was clever before by selecting a remote location in the middle of nowhere. But truthfully, there is nowhere more alone and isolating than this city. People are burdened with busy schedules and stacked one on top of the other, forcing them to ignore their neighbors for the sake of privacy. They don't want to know what I'm doing here; they just appreciate that I'm quiet and keep to myself.

I could be a Dahmer copycat, but as long as I'm severing heads quietly and making sure to keep the electricity on so the mutilated body parts don't reek up the hallway, people could care less.

As I approach Subject 9, I hold the syringe up and then, with clear warning in my gaze, order him to remain silent. "Let's make this quick. I have a date tonight."

Sweat beads his forehead. The duct tape is slick as I rip it away from his mouth.

He blows the mouthguard out, his ashen face highlighted with red welts and rashes from the adhesive. "Please...you have to let me go. I don't deserve this—this is insane."

I inhale a deep breath, acutely aware of the absent scent in the stale air, that intoxicating mix of coconut and bergamot.

Her scent.

The fragrance of my lab when she was there.

Blakely's scent imbued me, putting me right at her mercy.

Since smells travel directly to the memory and emotional hubs of the brain, even the absence of a smell can trigger an emotional response.

If I don't rectify us soon, I fear I'll completely lose the memory of it, and it will forever linger in that haunted cabin basement.

I slip my good hand into a glove and proceed with tightening the straps on my subject.

"God, no..." He fastens his eyes shut. "I haven't eaten for two days. This is inhumane!"

There's that word again, and just like every other time I've heard it uttered, the vertebrae along my spine locks taut. "Really, inhumane is how you subjected your college roommate to a hazing stunt that left him maimed for life. But—" I shove the mouthguard back into his mouth and secure it with a new strip of tape "—I'm neither your judge nor your jury."

And with the exact replication of the treatment, I won't be his executioner, either.

I'm going to cure this man.

The dial on the ECT machine is set to the precise voltage. The chemical compound is delivered in the exact manner. Anesthesia is not administered. Every single aspect is parallel to Blakely's procedure.

I strap the electrodes to the subject's temples in the bilateral ETC position and meet his eyes—eyes wide and glassy with fear, and a touch vacant with acceptance. Shallow affect doesn't allow for a wide range of emotions, yet even a psychopath can fear their own demise.

I toggle the switch, and his body stiffens, muscles contracting with the induced seizure. A dark pool spreads along the white cotton sheet covering his lower half as he wets himself. His eyes roll into the back of his head, showing only the bloodshot white, as he bucks against the gurney.

At the predetermined time mark, I kill the switch. His body sags in relief. After unhooking him from the machine, I set the timer on my phone for five hours. That's how long it took Blakely to come back to me. Even then, I carried her to the river and submerged her in cold water to fully revive her.

Haunting memories of that night return with a

vengeance, the procedure forcing me to recall every achingly beautiful and painful moment. The feel of her fiery lips crashing against mine amid the frigid waterfall as it rained down on us. The tears that streaked her cheeks when her emotions soared to shattering heights.

The razor-sharp knife of despair plunged into my chest at her rejection.

The denial of her feelings that, although gutted me emotionally, also wounded my ego.

Looking back now, it's so fucking clear. I should have called her out on her lies. I should have never let her go. I should have wrapped my arms around her and kissed her madly until her guarded walls came crashing down.

My fist slams into the metal table, and I only register the brief pain before blood seeps through the bandage.

I allowed her to manipulate my emotions, so I deserve my misery for being so weak.

If I had the clarity of hindsight, I would've told her the brutal truth: *Love makes us crazy, baby. Welcome to the land of the feeling.*

What Blakely doesn't understand is that her capacity to feel was always there, it was just untapped. And we did more than tap it—we opened Pandora's box. Maybe that did terrify me a little, made me question...everything.

I admit, I didn't take into account the impact such a phenomenal change would have. I couldn't have accounted for it; no one has ever succeeded where I have. There is no empirical data or test cases to compare. No warning labels.

She's different now, but still so much the same. What was always there is now heightened, the desire to inflict pain magnified. The dare to make others suffer amplified.

Blood calls to her.

It knows her name.

Killing is in her veins now.

As soon as I read the news article, I knew it was Blakely who sank a blade into Ericson. Not once, but thirteen times. The authorities labeled it overkill.

I won't be like you, Alex. I'm not a killer.

No, Blakely may have never become a killer. Her malady as a psychopath was never that of a murderer.

She's a justice dealer.

And who deserved a round of justice more than a putrid rapist like Ericson Daverns?

As her emotions and neural pathways are still equilibrating, her responses and reflexes are going to be erratic. She will be volatile one moment, lethargic the next. In time, she will let go of her guilt over taking a man's life. She will come to realize she had no other choice.

It was either him or her.

Although Ericson would've made a prime subject to further the experiment, his purpose was best served by allowing Blakely to explore her emotional range. A scientific sacrificial lamb.

Fortunately for me, there are other Ericsons in this world, a few of them located right here in this city. On that particular research, my beautiful monster has already done the vetting work for me.

A page torn right from her little black book.

Such as Subject 9 on my gurney. His name was third down on her "Douche checklist." Her own personal rating system, how she tallied her targets from the least deserving to the most deserving of a client's revenge. It's a vetted list of the worst kind of humans, and subsequently, the ones at the top happen to be psychopaths.

Her notes on the subject of psychopathy are particularly interesting. As she had a special insight into this disposition, she knew one revenge scheme wasn't suitable for all.

Like Reilly Stafford, her revenge for him was just, but he has a higher purpose now. He doesn't have to be a waste.

Reminded of my patient, I check his vitals. "You probably think I'm callous," I say to him, regardless of whether or not he can hear me. "That I exhibit similar psychopathic tendencies. You wouldn't be wrong. In order for one to achieve what I have, one has to assert a great level of insensitivity."

Feeling no pulse, I frown down at him. "But don't

forget that a psycho killer did put an icepick through my sister's brain. Something so traumatic does have a tendency to leave a mark." I push harder against his neck. He's unresponsive. I drop my hand.

Anger seizes my nerves, and I shove the gurney away. "Fuck."

With begrudging effort, I wheel the gurney to the kitchenette and raise the bed. The body slides off and lands with an unceremonious *flop* on the plastic sheet. Counter forensic measures are taken to clean the body and mask the burn marks on the temples, but only as an added precaution. No one will miss Reilly Stafford. He's a toxic dump of human filth.

I cover myself with a used Tyvek suit I fished from the same medical dumpsite I sourced the gurney, then I select the switchblade—the one identical to the blade Blakely used to carry on her person, the one she brutally stabbed Ericson thirteen times with.

I stand over the dead body and grip the hilt, then begin stabbing his chest and torso.

It's not an easy feat, driving a knife into a body. Without the presence of rage, you feel the blade slice past skin and cartilage and tendon. You have to wriggle the knife loose and pry it out. The sound is worse.

The time of death is so closely marked to the knife wounds, a medical examiner will find it difficult to determine that cause of death wasn't due to the attack. I make sure to hit the heart, and watch blood slowly ooze atop his chest.

I stab him twelve times, one less than Blakely's count, but authorities will still label it as overkill.

Even though it's not scientific in the least, when I chose my subjects from her list, I believed a link to Blakely would tip the scales in our favor, that the next treatment would be a success. How sentimentally superstitious of me.

But here I am once again, another failed procedure, another expired subject.

I could recreate the experiment a hundred times, do everything exactly identical, and I would never get the same outcome. I don't even have to compare the data to know why.

The result is unique to Blakely.

She is unique.

I'm unsure if this realization infuriates me or excites me—but it does simplify the objective.

For the past two years, I've been trying to change the world by designing a preventative. A cure to inhibit the decay and deterioration of the mind into a psychopathic state, when the cure is far more elaborate and…unique.

The objective has never been more clear.

I know what has to be done.

Once I dump the body, making sure to get every detail precise, it's time to find my little lost monster.

There is preparation to be done. The groundwork must be lain.

They say absence makes the heart grow stronger.

The anticipation is killer.

I had wanted to share my discovery, my breakthrough with the world. I had wanted to honor my sister and restore her status in the medical community.

Now I don't want to share Blakely with anyone.

It's not about prevention at all.

It's about elimination.

And I have the perfect calibrated weapon to carry out that objective.

OLD FLAMES

BLAKELY

*M*y plane touches down at eight-thirty on the west coast. The San Francisco airport teems with eager tourists, arriving in shorts and tanks and pasty skin anxious for a sunburn. It takes me half an hour of wandering the airport maze to get to the outside world, where a hot and humid blast of coastal air hits me like a wet blanket.

I Uber to the downtown hotel I rented for the night. Located only blocks from Union Square, the luxury hotel boasts views of the cityscape, the bay, Alcatraz, Golden Gate and the Bay Bridge. While the suite's terrace view is quite breathtaking, I'm here for none of that.

My phone pings with a text. I set my wineglass on the marble table and slide the message open. Tension knots my belly as I reply to the text, then call down to the lobby.

Before I ventured to Devil's Peak, I had sent an email to the renowned criminal psychologist Dr. London Noble. In vague reference to myself and without providing any names or identifying particulars, I detailed Alex's theory on psychopaths, his gruesome experiment, and the fact the convicted serial killer Grayson Sullivan had been the direct catalyst.

To be honest, the email sounded insane. I didn't expect a response from this woman, who has been through much of her own suffering at the hands of a deranged killer. So I was shocked when Dr. Noble invited me to speak with her in person.

I mean, I could've just scheduled a session with the psychologist. Shown up at her townhouse office and sprang the whole horror story on her right in her therapy room, using the doctor/patient confidentiality clause and demanding all her answers. And normally, that's exactly what I would have done. Treated her as an obstacle to be removed in order to obtain my objective. Quick. Easy. Direct.

I reach for the Cabernet, take a long sip, savoring the robust flavor and heated buzz rushing my veins. My fingertips turn white against the wineglass as my grip tightens.

I'm not the same *quick, easy, direct* woman. I second-guess every thought and decision, my emotions and brain at war with each other.

I feel fucking *crazy*, and I wonder if this is how women feel all the time. Questioning themselves, analyzing every damn thought, doubting their every choice.

If so, they have my fucking sympathy. No wonder most of my revenge-seeking clients were women.

A low knock sounds at the door. Two slow, light raps that ratchet my heart rate. I walk to the entrance and, rolling my shoulders back, slip into a new frame of mind and open the door.

Dr. Noble looks exactly like her professional picture online. Long dark hair braided over one shoulder. A sophisticated yet sexy black pencil skirt suit. Black-rimmed glasses. Refined and polished. Beautiful.

"Blakely Vaughn?" she asks with a serious expression that states why she's here.

I nod once. "Thank you for meeting with me, Dr. Noble. Please, come in." I step aside to allow her access.

As she enters the suite, she sets her leather handbag—Prada, I note—on the entryway table. "I prefer if you call me London. What we're about to discuss negates the need for formalities and polite etiquette."

I close the door. "Fair enough." I head straight for

the marble table and take a slug of wine, then raise the bottle toward her in offer. "Need a glass?"

A smile flits across her delicate lips. "I like that you inquire if I *need* instead of *want*. Very decisive. Says a lot about you."

In true shrink fashion, she doesn't actually answer the question. I pour her a big glass. "Analyzing me already."

She shrugs, unapologetic. "That's who I am." She accepts the wine. "So, who are you, Blakely?"

I set the bottle down with a resounding *clink* against the marble. "That's a damn good question."

Head canted, she studies me with drawn eyebrows. Then she takes a sip of wine before she seriously begins. "You were born a psychopath."

"Yes. A rather happy one."

"This doctor…" She moves toward the sofa, places her drink on the end table, and unbuttons her blazer before taking a seat. "I hesitate to regard him as such, but you said he's a biomedical scientist. He develops cures for diseases."

I inhale a deep breath. "Yes."

London crosses her legs slowly as her gaze assesses me. "He found your psychopathic nature to be a disease. And he…cured you."

"Yes," I say in confirmation.

"What you're claiming is impossible."

"And yet, here I am. The product of the good,

unhinged doctor." Smile tight, I add, "Because Grayson Sullivan murdered his sister."

"Interesting." Her expression is neutral, revealing no hint as to how the mention of her tormentor's name affects her.

In my email to her, I stated one of Grayson's victims was linked to Alex, but I didn't use any detailed descriptors or names. I'm still hesitant to give too much away now, but what I need can only be gleaned by an equal exchange of information.

"I'm sure you didn't have me fly across the country just to recount what I 'hypothetically' relayed in email." I take the seat across from her and mimic her body language. Woman to woman. "And I didn't fly across the damn country to recount it, either. I need to find the person who did this to me. And when I do, I need to know what makes him tick." I suppress a dark smile at my Alex pun.

She rubs the side of her palm, deep eyes regarding me. It's unnerving, the way she holds my gaze. Most people make eye contact then look away. It's rude to stare into a person's eyes too long. This is one of the first things I taught myself, so as not to make others feel uncomfortable.

Now I understand what it feels like to be regarded by a callous stare.

"And you believe I can somehow help you find this man," she states.

"I know you can."

"I'm not sure how."

"Alex's sister," I say, steeling my nerves to hold her intense stare. "You studied Sullivan. You were close to him. You know about his victims. Which means, you have information not known to the public about Dr. Mary Jenkins." I lift my chin higher. "I need this information."

For the first time since London entered the room, her mask slips and her features betray her. The widening of her eyes, the slight part of her mouth. This victim affects her. Maybe because Mary was a doctor, a sort of professional colleague. Maybe because of the gruesome manner in which Mary was murdered. A victim of her own barbaric lobotomy practice.

"Unfortunately, I was never given much information on Dr. Jenkins," she says, takes a sip of wine. "But let's drop all pretense, Blakely. Finding Alex is only partly why we're here. There's something else you want, and I'm not sure why you think I can help you get it."

Anxiety worms beneath my skin, my patience thin. How much of the truth can I reveal to her? Confess that I killed a man? That I can't turn myself in because, selfishly, I don't want to wither away in prison? That I have to correct this defect inside me first so I can do hard time?

Just the absurdity of my thoughts makes me nearly crack into hysterical laughter.

"He tortured me," I say instead. "He experimented on my brain. He injected me with…I don't even know what he put inside me, and now I'm this…" I trail off, frustration polluting my thoughts. "I'm this other person."

London leans forward. "Take three deep breaths."

A manic laugh slips free, the insult sharp. "I never used to have to take fucking breaths." But I do. I pause long enough to breathe and compose myself. "I don't even recognize myself. It's like waking up in someone else's skin every day, and it's disorienting, terrifying. I don't just want to find him; I want to carve out his damn heart. Douse him in gasoline and set him aflame." *Make him suffer the fire that should've been his fate.* My hands curl into fists. "I want revenge."

Even as I confess this, as I voice my desire to the universe, I feel the omission in my words. And Dr. Noble is good at what she does—she senses it, too.

"Passion is a complex beast," she says, her voice resolute. "It can present in many different forms. Anger, fear, desperation, vengeance, obsession. Love." Her gaze traps mine. "And the tricky part is, it's usually a combination of all."

My nails bite into my palms. The confusing and complicated emotions I feel for Alex twists me daily. I don't need this woman pointing them out. I don't need another doctor fucking with my head. I know I'm sick.

He *made* me sick.

Incensed, I shake my head. "I have one motive, and that's to force him to correct the damage he's caused and reverse the procedure, and if he can't—" I shrug, letting the silence underscore the blank. "The world has no use for a monster like him."

"You want him to reverse the treatment," she says.

"More than anything."

"What if that's not a possibility? What then?"

"Then, like I said. I'll do what I do best. Take my revenge."

"But then you still have to wake up every day as who you are now," she says, applying infuriating logic. "You know, Blakely, there's another possibility as to why this might be happening to you."

I exhale a heavy breath and reach for my wineglass. "London, I'm not trying to be difficult, as I appreciate your time, but honestly, psychiatry has never worked for me."

"That's good, then, as I'm not a psychiatrist." Her smile is disarming. "As you pointed out, I worked closely with Grayson Sullivan and others like him. I've studied the psychopathic mind, as I'm sure you've devoted countless hours of study to psychopathy when you understood what you were."

"Of course," I say.

"Then I wonder if you've ever heard of disempathetic type." At the confused draw of my eyebrows, she leans forward. "There is some debate about this in the psychiatric community, but it's where a psychopath has a restricted circle of empathy for those closest to them. In other words, it's possible to develop a deep, emotional bond or connection for another person, if only limited."

"That sounds like a fairy tale for my kind."

London nods. "That's what most say."

"But you think it's possible, and that I've somehow developed intense feelings for Alex." Simply saying his name triggers an ache in my chest. "That's more like Stockholm. The only thing I feel for him is deep, emotional disdain."

"Have you ever been close, truly close, with anyone in your life before?"

I consider her question seriously. "No. Never." I hold up my hand to halt her next question. "But have you ever diagnosed a disempathetic type?"

She pushes back in the sofa, her shoulders relaxing. "In fact I have, Grayson." She pauses a beat to let me absorb this information. "Or rather, he diagnosed himself. Then he told me I needed to master my passions." A curious glimmer flashes in her eyes. "He was offended I refused to consider the possibility for him at first. But in the end, I conceded that Grayson did harbor the capability to care and even protect those he deemed worthy."

The way she refers to him on a first name basis doesn't escape me. "Did he consider you worthy?"

"I think he did."

"So his deep, emotional connection to you resulted in him kidnapping you. Forcing you to watch him commit murder. Nearly killing you…"

"As bizarre as my experiences with Grayson were, yes. To a highly intelligent and damaged individual such as he was, his emotional capability was entirely unique to him. He was capable of love, in his own way."

Curious. I tilt my head. "He was in love with you." It's not a question, but the inquisitive tone of my voice is evident.

"He believed he was," she answers honestly, and I appreciate her candidness with me. "But what is love but simply chemicals in the brain that make us believe in our feelings?"

My defenses lower a notch. I'm exhausted trying to keep them in place. "I'm sorry, London, for bringing up what happened. Saying you've been through hell is a pathetic understatement, and it's not my intention to question your experiences."

"Would you have apologized before?" she asks bluntly.

I huff a derisive laugh. "No."

"Then don't apologize now. If I wasn't able to talk about my experiences, then I'd be a hypocrite for asking my patients to do so."

And suddenly, I like Dr. London Noble.

"Understood." I shake my head as I pivot back to the

origin of this conversation. "I might consider this disempathetic thing, but my emotions aren't only centered around one person. Since trying to reassimilate back into my life, I'm overwhelmed with emotions all the time. It's exhausting and, honestly, I'm a little terrified I'm actually going crazy."

She considers my statement in earnest. "Relationships are complicated, Blakely. The mind is very complex. It's not black and white. Gray matter isn't psychopathic or non-psychopathic. There are varying shades along the spectrum. Change is happening every second, in every facet of our lives. Just because you thought yourself incapable of empathy and love before, doesn't mean you would be incapable forever."

My heart roars inside my chest. *Relationship* is a weak and insulting way to describe what is between Alex and me. Even if I admit I'm capable of change, even if I accept that my "experience" brought on extreme emotions which impacted my psyche, there's no way in hell I'm acknowledging that a relationship, a *connection*, with Alex is what altered my brain chemistry.

Because that's what she's suggesting. That I'm some sort of enchanted psychopath and Alex is my Prince Charming.

We are not a fairy tale.

We're a horror story.

"Even if I'm now capable of love, it wouldn't be for

him. Passion isn't a beast, he's the beast," I say. "I won't hold my breath waiting for him to transform into a prince. That's delusional."

She makes an amused sound of understanding. "It's not waiting for the beast to transform into a prince and save us. It's about uncovering the terrifying beast within ourselves and—"

"Confronting it?"

"No, making it stronger and more terrifying than our fear so we can conquer that which weakens us."

I hold her unyielding gaze, her meaning settling deep in my bones.

Alex does weaken me, but not in the assumed way —and London understands this.

However, as much as I appreciate her insight, these aren't the answers I came here to get. "I understand what you're saying, but I can't...I don't accept he's the catalyst. I was one way before Alex subjected me to his torture treatment. Now I'm different, altered. It's just that simple, Dr. Noble."

She sits forward and reaches across to take my hand. I pull back at first, startled.

"Let me feel your pulse."

With a resigned breath, I place my hand against hers, and her fingers rest over my wrist.

"Alex," she says.

My pulse jumps in my veins. I remove my hand

from her touch. "A parlor trick that only proves how much I loathe him."

London eases back in her seat. "I would love to dive deeper with you. Explore your emotional range with psychotherapy. Obviously, I'm fascinated on a professional level to find out more about the cure you underwent, but I also believe I can help you."

I jerk my head, tossing my hair from my eyes. "Alex's 'cure' isn't the word I'd use for this disturbed affliction. Besides, he didn't make me aware of the process. He kept much of it from me. I can't tell you any more than what I've already revealed in the email. And I believe the only way you can help is by giving me the information I came here for so I can find the bastard."

A tight-rimmed smile lines her mouth. "Dr. Jenkins was a narcissist with a god complex. Grayson stalked her. Witnessed her brutality and total callous disregard for her patients. It's hard to say whether or not Dr. Jenkins was committed to her lobotomy procedures in the name of discovery or her own selfish endeavors, as I never assessed her myself.

"But…," London adds, "Grayson did talk about her once during a session. He said the way she disposed of her victims was the most telling of all about her. Instead of falsifying their death record, hiding the evidence of her malpractice and allowing the families to have closure by burying their loved ones, she relocated them to a remote location and disposed of them herself. She simply made them disappear, their lives of no more consequence to her than a dead animal."

My skin prickles, the hairs at the nape of my neck lift away. I know where Mary buried her victims, because I've seen the graveyard. I've felt the bones. I assumed they were Alex's victims, and maybe some of them are, but I know intrinsically that his sister was the first to dig up that earth.

The question now becomes if whether or not Alex was aware of his sister's disposal practices, if that's why he ultimately chose her cabin, or if it was a sick coincidence.

Like sister, like brother.

"She sounded ruthless, heartless," I say, trying to mask the anxiousness in my voice. I'm omitting a lot of details from this conversation, but it's necessary to keep London in the dark for my own sake. Maybe one day, when this horrible nightmare is over, I'll tell her more. I'll let her analyze me and try to help. Then, maybe she can.

But this is my sickness. Alex is my sickness. And I greedily want him all to myself.

"Did Grayson ever say anything about Mary's ties to her brother?" I ask.

London inclines her head. "If Grayson knew of Alex's existence, he didn't factor him into his plans for his sister. That's all I can offer." Her gaze drills into me, unnerving. "What I've said here is rather unethical, but I feel for your plight, so I trust it will remain between us, an informational *quid pro quo*."

There is some threat there, a vague demand for me to give her a secret she can hold against me so we're on equal ground.

"Of course," I say. "This conversation never happened."

"Thank you."

"Alex made it seem like he and his sister were close…" I trail off, searching my memories of our conversations. "I wish I knew a way to draw him out."

The watch feels heavy in my pocket all of a sudden, its secrets burning to be told.

"You're looking for an Achilles' heel, a weak spot. Something to use as leverage. But I think you've failed to see that you've already found the biggest leverage of all."

I shake my head. "I don't understand."

"You don't have to worry about tracking him down or drawing him out. You're his creation, his masterpiece. If he truly believes he cured you, that he achieved his greatness through you, he'll come for you, Blakely."

My breath stalls in my lungs.

Her words feel ominous.

When I didn't recover his remains at the cabin, that only confirmed what my instincts already knew: Alex has been watching me. He's likely been in my apartment, where he could've copied my black notebook—and used the names listed there for his own nefarious purpose.

Two of my revenge targets have already wound up dead.

No—not *wound up*. Murdered. Caleb Foster and Christopher Monroe were murdered.

Revealing that to London would tip the *quid pro quo* scales, however.

"I hope you're right," I say to her. "I want him to come for me. I'm not afraid of him." I conceal the tremble of my knee by crossing my legs. It's not Alex I fear, the trepidation of what he may do to me.

It's the fear of what I'm capable of. If I continue on this course, I could become just like him.

A flash of Ericson's pained face. The switchblade in my hand. The red covering my palms.

"No. I don't believe you're fearful of him," London says, breaking into my thoughts. "But fear, true fear you've never experienced before, felt on such a visceral level... Well, it can make you unpredictable. And for a person who has only ever experienced shallow affect, who has always been in control of their low range emotions, I think that unpredictability frightens you more than you may admit to yourself."

I'm silent for a long moment, the sounds of the city drifting in through the cracked terrace doors. There's a whole world out there full of emotion and sensation and it feels overwhelming. If I don't confront Alex, if he doesn't correct what he's done…

"I'm scared I'll lock myself away," I blurt. "That if I go on like this, I won't be able to cope, that it will continue to become too much. That I'll just go mad."

"However it came to be, you're a different creature now. You have to learn to embrace your emotions. That's the only way."

I reach for my wine and take a lingering sip. "Dulling them helps a little."

Her smile is genuine. "As does masking them with one of the easiest feelings to master. Hatred."

At her intense stare, I set the glass down and fold my hands in my lap. "I do hate him," I say, my voice laced with steely venom. "I've never hated another person before in my life. Well, except for Kyle Sellars. A bully from grade school."

"And how did you handle him?" she probes.

I cock my head. "I buried his face in an ant bed."

London nods slowly. "A psychopath with violent tendencies," she remarks, but it's the curious gleam in her gaze that sets my nerves on edge. "Interesting."

"Self-defense," I say, in way of explanation. I've never felt the need to explain my actions before.

"Self-preservation is also why you're here. It will be very interesting to see how you handle Alex."

I swipe the back of my hand across my forehead, the

wine heating my skin. "Out of curiosity, how would Grayson go about handling Alex?"

London wets her lips, and I swear there's a spark in her golden eyes. She's more than professionally intrigued with her patient; she's fascinated by him. "He would subject him to his own course of treatment." She tilts her head, her gaze never leaving mine. "But that's only if Alex proved to be deserving of such a punishment."

I don't know why I say it; I've never sought approval from anyone in my life. But for some reason, I want this woman to understand what I have to do and why.

"He's a killer. I wasn't his first subject."

"I see." She laces her fingers together on her lap. "That is unfortunate."

"As demented as this may come across, I wish Grayson was around to reap vigilante justice on Alex."

"One should always be careful what they wish for." Her eyes flash. "If Grayson was around, my patient would probably approve of your pursuit. He would find it…distasteful to interfere. As long as you were successful, he'd have no reason to hunt Dr. Chambers."

"Once upon a time, vengeance was my ethos. I plan to be successful."

"Then, all I can offer you is my hope that you find what you need. Oh, and this." She stands and grabs her bag from the table, then places her business card on the sofa arm near me. "My personal line is on the back. Should you change your mind about engaging in sessions. I really am interested in working with you, Blakely."

There's a weighted beat where I stare at her card, at her slender fingers next to it, as if she's waiting for me to accept the invitation. My gaze lingers on the faded ink of a tattooed key along the side of her palm before she pulls her hand away.

"Thank you for all your help, London." I cast a look upward to meet her eyes once more.

Her smile seems sincere.

As she heads toward the door, I cross to the terrace and gaze out over the city. I pull Alex's broken watch from my pocket and rub the smooth pewter surface, a strange sensation unfurling through me as I hear London leave the hotel room. I never mentioned Alex's last name. Yet, near the end of our conversation, she referred to him as Dr. Chambers.

I'm not sure what that means, but it unspools a thread of apprehension between us.

I click the watch closed.

Despite my wariness, London knows her psychopaths. If I'm to trust her observation, then I don't need to waste any more time searching for Alex.

He will come for me.

And this time, I'll be ready.

4

STRONGEST SENSE

ALEX

*T*he captivating scent of coconut soaks into my pores, arousing my senses. I rub the rich emulsion of Blakely's body wash between my fingers and thumb, savoring the indulgent feel as I imagine her soaping her body, hands massaging the lather into her wet, silky skin, fingertips exploring between her thighs, washing sudsy water over her breasts.

I'm a man painfully consumed as I stand within her glass-encased shower, rock-hard and aching, like a deranged stalker. These temptations are dangerous. The craving makes me lose sight of my purpose.

I dab the body wash on the bandage covering my hand to take her scent with me, as if I'm not tortured enough. I wipe the remainder off on the green towel hung on the wall hook, then straighten it to appear as if it was never disturbed.

The fine art of breaking-and-entering in NYC is all about confidence, and not looking like a pathetic creep. Wait patiently for the right person to arrive outside the building. Smile at the nice elderly lady as you time your passing just right. Offer to help carry groceries to her apartment. Don't accept the dollar tip she offers. The unassuming cardigan and glasses help. Leave the way you came, waiting until she disappears inside her apartment to sneak into the emergency staircase.

Not the most tactful or discreet method, but a method that will draw the least amount of attention, and one that has worked for me before.

As I've already picked the lock on her apartment door several times, I knew how long it would take. I'm still surprised she hasn't invested in an alarm system. It's as if she's still trying to maintain her previous life, one where she's the predator and not the prey.

Which means there's a possibility she hasn't made the connection yet.

One of the targets from her client list brutally murdered is a tragedy.

But two reported murdered so closely together and in the same manner is not a coincidence.

Blakely won't be able to deny her suspicions for long. She may be doubting her own mind due to the battle with her emotions, but she's too intelligent not to make the connection.

Which means, I'm running short on time to observe her. She's always been clever and resourceful. Soon, she'll get her answers. The anticipation makes my hands tremble.

I'm missing the thrill that stirs my blood from watching her, if only from a distance. Because that was the bargain I struck with my inner devil.

Patience was never my strong suit.

When she didn't return last night, the obsessive monster within me went wild, rattling the cage, demanding to find her.

What if something happened? What if she's hurt?

What if she snapped and has done something worse?

The darker my fears go, the more desperate I feel. I have no choice; I have to protect her.

My desire to inhale her scent once more quenched, I leave the bathroom and head upstairs to the loft, seat myself behind her metal desk and open her laptop. I plunder through her calendar where nothing of importance stands out, then I read through her email.

There's a confirmation notice for a flight booked to San Francisco.

Alarm drums inside my chest. I flex my hand over the keys to steady my nerves. What is a city girl doing in California? What or *who* could she possibly be meeting?

I check the itinerary for the flight. She's scheduled to return to LaGuardia tomorrow evening. I push back and stare at the screen, my brain conjuring theories as to why Blakely would need to take such a sudden and unexpected trip.

There are no other messages or scheduled appointments. Just a roundtrip ticket and a menacing feeling crackling the air. Fixated on the location, the fiend in me won't stop here. I do a deep dive into her data and scour deleted emails, unearthing one I can tell she tried to keep buried.

Fury ignites my blood as I read an email sent to Dr. Noble. She was the criminal psychologist assigned to Grayson Sullivan before his trial. She gets murderers off of death row and reduced sentences. And the things Blakely tells her—private, personal things between us— I slam the laptop shut.

Betrayal is a whip sliced right through my soul, if such a thing exists.

What possible reason could Blakely have for involving her? Sullivan brutally murdered my sister, and Dr. Noble, to be honest, is less than a degree better. What answer is Blakely seeking—?

As soon as the thought occurs, something akin to guilt punches my stomach. For all my intelligence, I suddenly feel the dullest haze of sublime stupidity. Of course she's reaching out to any link tied to me. Of course she'd uncover the common denominator between herself and Sullivan.

I opened the pathways of her brain to a whole new experience, one heightened and volatile and frightening, and then, when I didn't return for her, I abandoned her. Left her to fend for herself in a confused state.

I picture Blakely through the flames as they engulf the cabin interior—that image of her seared into my memory, a nightmare I can't wake from. I relive it over and over, the moment our eyes met across the fire, the split second where I questioned her choice as the pained expression tore at her features.

I should have leapt through the flames for her.

If I could wind back time, I would never have let her go.

"Shit." Now she's seeking answers from the one source that could destroy us.

I need to know what psychobabble Dr. Noble is feeding her. What she plans to do with the information Blakely has so blatantly and irresponsibly supplied to her about me and my project.

I need to pay my own visit to Dr. Noble.

As I head toward the stairs, I spy Blakely's open bedroom area, and I can't resist the temptation. Her bed is right there. Unmade. Covers bunched in the center. I can envision her curled into them, her arms hugging her pillow, soft tresses of blond hair falling over her face.

Then, as I close the distance, my gaze snags on

something white balled up beneath her pillow. I extract the material and hold it out to examine.

I recognize the shirt right away, because it's one of mine.

Blakely sleeps with my T-shirt.

A devious flare of arousal courses my blood, going straight to my groin. I bring the fabric to my nose and inhale, recognizing the scent of my cologne. I smile.

She may picture my face when she's jabbing a punching bag, but she clings to my scent at night when she's fearful, when she needs comfort—and that knowledge is powerful.

I tuck the shirt beneath the pillow where it belongs.

As I descend the loft, my senses pick up on something out of place. Standing at the base of the staircase, I keep my back to the kitchen and scan the living area, noting every detail. The front door is closed. Locked. The apartment is quiet, but there's a draft.

Too late, I catch the flutter of linen curtains and the open window.

I turn toward the kitchen, and he's already standing before me.

My skin ices over. Every artery inside my body seizes. My heart beats manically in my chest, trying to force blood flow, but my mind is overriding basic bodily functions as I stare into the cold eyes of a killer.

Grayson Sullivan.

The Angel of Maine.

The monster who murdered my sister.

"You," I say, my voice some distant construct of my thoughts.

Sullivan lifts his chin, pale eyes boring into me with menacing intent. "Dr. Alex Chambers. You've been very busy making a mess."

Confusion draws my features tight, but I don't get the chance to question him. We both move instantaneously. I go for his middle, he aims for my face.

Amid the violent clash, I lose consciousness.

The room goes dark.

Blakely's scent is the last thing to fade from my senses.

5

ANGEL OF MERCY

ALEX

*O*f all the structures and systems in the universe, time is the cruelest.

Our whole life is centered around time. Our day comprised of its relative nature. Too much time as we sit bored in a waiting room, letting time waste away like it's not preciously finite. Waiting for the clock to run out at the end of the year so we can reboot and start over fresh, a whole new person with dreams and goals.

In the same vein, there is never enough time to complete an important task, a goal, a dream. And deeper still is the loss of time, those feelings of regret, or the desperate ache of too little time when last moments are spent with loved ones before their time is gone forever.

The time I've expended studying Grayson Sullivan could constitute as obsessive, and should serve me now. It should have prepared me for the moment he materialized in my life. Thinking over my course, it was inevitable we would cross paths. Yet the cruel irony is when faced with our deepest desire, preparation is often the biggest miscalculation of time.

I could never prepare myself for this moment.

And now I have no choice but to wait, seconds turning into minutes, as I'm strapped to my own gurney. To illustrate my point, a faint *tick*, *tick*, *tick* whispers through the air, a mocking sound dredged to the surface from a delusion. There are no clocks here—I made damn sure.

When I awoke, bleary-eyed and groggy, the bitter aftertaste of some drug coating my tongue, the memory of him subduing me started to filter back. My head thumps painfully from where I was hit with a metal bar, and I can feel the puncture wound in my neck from a needle.

I'm fighting dehydration. My temples pulse with an angry thud. As my mind clears, I feel the leather restraints strapped across my forehead, wrists, and ankles.

The ticking fades away at the sound of boots walking across the floor. I try to turn my head, immediately sending a sharp pain up my neck. "How did you get me here?"

There are other, more pressing questions that need answers, but let's start here. You can't carry a full-grown man around the city without garnering some attention.

There's the clatter of tools on the metal table, then Grayson moves into my line of sight. He's wearing a black thermal and black pants. Those piercing colorless eyes assess me coolly with indifference.

"Wheeling an unconscious man down the sidewalk isn't a red flag in this city. I think I even waved to a cop on my way here."

Sullivan is talking to me. Hearing his voice is a shock to my system. I've seen him on countless TV stations, dug up rare interviews on the Internet. But this is different; there is no mask.

I'm looking into the soulless eyes of a psychopathic killer with no empathy or mercy.

I hold his penetrating gaze as my mind quickly calculates the logic of this situation.

He knew where my improvised lab was located. That means he's been watching me for at least a couple of days if not more. He followed me to Blakely's apartment. There's an uncertain variable where I don't know if Dr. Noble apprised her patient of certain details, or whether his knowledge was gleaned from stalking his doctor, but Blakely's email was sent out days before Dr. Noble replied. Grayson could've intercepted that missive. Blakely may not have even met with Dr. Noble—he may have intercepted her.

Either scenario concludes one crucial truth that can't be ignored.

He knows about Blakely.

Suddenly getting free of this gurney is vital.

I have to keep Grayson talking. I have to stay conscious. Which is going to be a difficult feat as I watch him systematically lay out tools—scalpel, electrodes, syringe—next to the gurney. He toggles on my electroconvulsive machine before reaching for a mouthguard.

Fuck.

"I couldn't have devised a better death for you myself," he says, selecting the electrode rods. "You should be proud, Dr. Chambers. This is all you, your hard work. A healer rarely gets to reap the benefit of his own methods."

He moves toward me with the mouthguard, and despite knowing it's useless to fight, to try to escape, as I always tell my subjects, my base survival instinct kicks in and I struggle against the restraints.

"Wait—" I say, trying to stall him. "If you kill me, then you can never recreate the treatment for yourself."

He stands over me. Something like amusement flashes behind his eyes. "I think you missed a glaringly obvious flaw in your treatment plan, doctor."

I swallow to moisten my dry throat. "What's that?"

"The catch twenty-two." He bears down on my wounded hand, and I groan out in pain. He shoves the guard into my mouth and seals a strip of duct tape over it. "For a psychopath to be cured, they first have to want the treatment. However, without the emotional capacity to care, there is no desire to be cured. A conundrum that renders your procedure impractical and useless."

Grayson stares down at me as he places the rods to my temples. I sink my teeth into the guard. He never looks away as he reaches over and turns on the juice, not gauging the voltage before electricity courses my body.

The induced seizure cords every muscle tight. My body planks against the gurney. My vision blurs, the tremors rattling my optic nerves. An overwhelming urge to vomit burns my esophagus, but I choke it back so I don't asphyxiate.

The session may only last a few seconds, but time is my enemy in this moment, and the seconds drag out as pain afflicts every cell in my body.

By the time Grayson kills the switch, I'm tunneling under.

A violent slap to my cheek rouses me back to consciousness. The tape is torn away, and the mouthguard falls to the gurney from my slack mouth.

"If your subjects can withstand a harder dose," Grayson says, "then surely the scientist can take a few small jolts."

I can't process a thought through the cloud of confusion. The acrid scent of seared flesh burns my nostrils. The memory of Blakely shooting me with a Taser rises to the surface of my thoughts, and I think I smile.

"Water," I manage to croak.

Silence answers back. After a few agonizing minutes where I fade in and out of awareness, I'm doused with a splash of tepid water over my face.

I lick my lips, ignoring the burning sensation at my temples. As more of the fog lifts, I test the leather cuff around my right wrist. The seizure loosened it a fraction.

"So this is…what," I say, hoping to keep him talking long enough to wriggle my arm free. "Punishment? The Angel of Maine is here to judge me, to turn my crimes against me?" A laugh escapes, sounding faraway in my ringing ears. This is what he does—makes his victims question themselves. Throws their sins in their face, forcing them to stare into their own black souls. "You can't make a man suffer for actions he doesn't regret."

I see Grayson approach from the corner of my eye. He rolls my lab chair close to the gurney and sits. I can feel his stare on the side of my face.

"I dislike that moniker," he says, a warning in his tone. "I'm not here to punish you, Chambers. You're doing that all by yourself, pining after a woman who loathes you." He releases a sardonic breath. "I've been watching your pathetic life for three days now, and I feel like I'm doing you a favor by putting you out of your misery."

The mention of Blakely flares my fried nerves. "Don't even think about her."

He *tsks*. "You should never reveal your weakness so easily."

I yank at the restraints, and the right cuff slackens even more. He didn't tighten it down enough.

"But no, I'm not here to punish you," he says. "I'm not that magnanimous. I don't give a shit about how many people you've killed or who your victims were. I'm here to stop you from making a bigger mess than you already have."

He flips through one of my journals and turns the page around so I can see. "It took me all of half a day to track you down. Serial killing one-oh-one: never work off of a list."

The page he's displaying is the list of names from Blakely's little black book.

"If the very savvy detective working these cases links you to these murders, then he can link me." He closes the journal. "Seeing as Dr. Mary Jenkins was your sister, one of my victims, it's not a huge leap from one killer to the next. From you to me." His gaze darkens. "You can understand why I can't let that happen. I have more than myself to protect." He stands to loom over me, and I notice the syringe in his hand.

The barrel is filled with my compound. I can tell by the color and consistency.

"While you were knocked out, I read through your notes. Interesting project, curing psychopaths. All because of me. I'm flattered." He sticks the needle in my arm, thumb poised over the plunger. "I wonder if we can reverse the process, fry your neural pathways until you're just like me."

Breath measured, I stare at the syringe. "You're smart enough to know it doesn't work like that."

His mouth tips into a disturbing smile. "That's disappointing. I guess we can just pump this poison in your veins and watch you swallow your tongue, instead."

My reflexes are dull, but with strength I barely feel, I pry my wrist free of the cuff and reach under the gurney. I always have a contingency plan. In the event a subject gets loose, I keep a scalpel taped beneath the bed. I never thought I'd have to use it—but I never thought I'd be at the mercy of a deranged killer, either.

In a thwarted heartbeat, I have the razor-sharp blade held to Grayson's neck.

Within the same beat, I feel the distinct tip of cold steel at my throat. I expel a shaky breath as Grayson holds a scalpel to my neck.

Locked in mirrored positions, we stare at one another. Waiting. Weapons gripped tight.

The water beads on my skin to mix with sweat, and

a tremor rolls through my arm. I'm still too weak from the electroshock, but I won't let him know this. "I should sever your carotid for what you did to my sister."

Grayson merely looks intrigued. "You could, or you could thank me. She wouldn't be in your life without me, otherwise."

She referring to the only woman in my life that means anything now. "Said like a true psychopathic narcissist."

I try not to let him inside my head, try to shut out his invasive voice, but his claim ignites my chest. I clench the scalpel in a tense fist, muscles strained.

"You had no other reason for taking my twin sister from this world," I say, "from taking her from *me*, than your own selfish, twisted compulsions."

"And I bet that just tears the wound wide open."

"Give me a reason," I demand.

Reason at least provides logic. Something I can assess, measure, comprehend.

Without reason, we're no better than animals. Beasts that tear each other apart for flesh and blood.

He narrows his eyes curiously. "Dr. Jenkins was a parasite," he says, his voice devoid of any emotion, as if he's simply stating a fact. "Her ego destroyed her long before I put an icepick through her skull. But that's not why you're here, stalking a woman you tortured. Your lust for revenge died the moment she flew into your orbit. So put your pathetic attempt to inflate your ego away. It's weak."

Blood roars in my ears. Every charged cell in my body wants to destroy him.

And yet, despite my indignant response to his assertion, I'm furious that he's right. My project stopped being about trying to avenge my sister and restore her name, and became all about my obsession with Blakely.

With forced conviction, I ease the blade of the scalpel away from his neck. A hairline bead of red remains on his skin. The overworked muscles of my forearm seize, and I drop the scalpel. It clatters loudly as it hits the floor between us.

"You at least owe me a quick death," I say.

Amusement lights his features. "A martyr killer," he says, lowering his own weapon. "I believe that's an oxymoron."

The strap across my forehead slackens as my neck relaxes. "It was never my intention to take a life."

"Lives," he corrects. Then he removes the needle from my arm, placing the syringe on the gurney. "After one failed attempt, you couldn't stop."

I don't miss his distinction between *didn't* and *couldn't*. I didn't have the choice to stop; I couldn't have stopped the pursuit of my project for anyone.

Until her.

"It's the ripple effect," I say. "Theoretically, it was

your actions that killed my subjects. They should be counted toward your victim pool."

He raises his chin, watching me with stone-cold eyes. "*Choice* killed your subjects. Your choice."

I turn my head away and stare at the dilapidated and stained ceiling. "So is this my punishment or confession?" I ask, my tone thick with sarcasm.

"You will find no absolution here." Grayson rolls the chair closer and makes himself comfortable, despite his words. "You have one chance to convince me why I shouldn't throw the switch on this crude machine and walk away, letting you fry to a crisp."

A sense of strange irony fills me. I should be quaking with fear, knowing the countdown on my clock is almost up. Grayson doesn't spare his victims. He's here to tie up a loose end, a variable he couldn't have predicted when he killed my sister.

My actions forced him to hunt me quickly, not giving him adequate time to observe me, to develop a punishment tailored to my "sins". Therefore, he wants me to provide the details for my own torturous death.

A mocking laugh slips out. "I didn't think you were a liar."

He doesn't respond. He doesn't have to.

Maybe it would be amusing to retrace my fumbling steps that brought me here. Why not? My last seconds should be given to Blakely, recounting our time together.

"Initially," I say, "it was all for Mary. I was devoted to my purpose, to restore what you destroyed."

"My psychologist would say you dissociated. Because deciding to experiment on people in the name of science, that's right out of a Mary Shelley novel."

"Oh, and torturing them with medieval devices for your own sick need is completely rational." I turn my head to see a dark smile slant his mouth.

"We all have sick needs to fulfill," he says. "Don't fool yourself."

An image of Blakely in the stairwell of my cabin flashes to mind. Shirt parted open, exposing the delicate swell of her breasts. Her green eyes large and imploring. Her body trembling beneath my exploratory touch.

Despite my ethical convictions that she was my subject, I craved her so badly it drove me mad.

I decide not to argue his point. "The project evolved. It became about needing to cure her for myself. So she could…" *Love me* sounds painfully pathetic, even if it's true. "So she could have the capability to love."

A curious expression crosses his face. "You're in love with your subject."

"I am, and it's maddening. I needed to know beyond any doubt that the treatment worked. I needed verifiable proof that she's capable of reciprocating my feelings. This is why I needed to duplicate the results on another subject, to have confirmation."

Grayson tilts his head. "You might be the most

delusional twist I've ever encountered, Chambers. Even if your insane experiment worked, that's the worst possible outcome. There's no way in hell this woman will feel anything but disdain for you after what you've done to her." He releases a low chuckle. "You had more of a chance when she was a psychopath."

"You know nothing about her."

"I know human nature."

"You're highly intelligent, Sullivan, but I doubt you worked out all the nuances of the human condition all on your own."

A heated flare ignites his eyes. A slight tic in his jaw.

A smile curls my lips. "You're still in contact with your psychologist," I say, working out the connection. "I've read about Dr. Noble. She's very insightful. And not just that, she gave you information on me. Why?"

Even as I ask the question, the pieces start to come together. At his refusal to answer, I say, "It appears I'm not the only one pining for a woman out of my reach."

Grayson's expression closes off. "You may be a skilled scientist, but this is one area you shouldn't dissect too closely."

"I'm a dead man anyway, right? You came here to kill me. Indulge my curiosity."

He pushes his thermal sleeves up, revealing the scars and tattoos that cover his arms. I'm drawn to the artwork, the puzzle pieces, questioning what they represent.

"There are consequences for our actions," Grayson says, rolling the chair forward. "Every action has a reaction. That's your science. You set your death into motion. Whether it's by my hand or another."

"What does that mean?"

"You can't kill a man like Ericson Daverns without major fallout."

A sick feeling gnaws at my stomach. I calculate all the angles, what I might have missed, what I didn't analyze or configure.

It doesn't shock me that he's drawn his own educated conclusions, but he didn't point the finger directly at Blakely. He's not entirely sure who killed Ericson.

I have more than one reason for selecting my subjects from her book of revenge, and that's to protect her. If she ever tries to turn herself in, the connection to the other murders—ones I plan to pin on a more believable subject—will discredit her claim.

I just need the murder weapon.

"Brewster," I say in response to his statement. Ericson's dirty client. The man with more seedy ties in this city than the mob.

I lost track of this player and didn't consider him any type of threat once Ericson's case was suspected as a mugging. What I failed to consider was how much money Ericson moved for his client—how much money Brewster potentially lost when his financial adviser was suddenly taken out of existence.

This puts Blakely in danger.

Grayson crosses his arms, a knowing look on his face. "For a man of so specific calculations, you're extremely narrow when considering your variables."

That might be the biggest insult he's delivered against me so far.

"Why are you telling me this?"

"Maybe I hold a small measure of respect for you. Or maybe I pity you." He stands to hover over the gurney. "I know how a woman can twist your head."

There's a scathing slight on the tip of my tongue about his psychologist, but I swallow it down. If I don't get free, then Blakely is either at the mercy to this fiend, or Brewster.

Neither of those scenarios will happen.

Grayson glances around my lab. "I noticed you have some sick hard-on for clocks," he says. "It's strange that you don't have any here."

"I'm trying to break a bad habit," I say, my tone flat.

He nods slightly, weighing some thought, before he looks down at me. "What would you do with more time, Dr. Chambers?"

I hold his measuring gaze, knowing this is a trick question, but I have to answer regardless.

"I'd protect the woman I love," I say honestly.

"That's vague."

I shake my head against the bedding, becoming increasingly more agitated by the restraints limiting my mobility. "I'd frame Brewster for the murders."

Since the second he revealed Brewster as a dangerous variable, the plan was already formulating. Brewster has a connection to Ericson. It wouldn't be difficult to find other connections between this man and Blakely's other revenge targets—or to create them.

Knowing his reputation, Brewster is likely already being monitored by a government entity, and time is already working against him. The right people just need concrete evidence.

I can offer them that.

Blakely would be safe, and Grayson would then have no reason to eliminate either of us. He'd no longer be connected to any of the murders.

"Two birds, one stone," I say, a cliché oversimplification of my plan.

He seems to appreciate this as his eyebrow arches in approval. He picks up the scalpel and sets it aside on the metal table. "So we're very clear, this offer of time isn't for you. I like games. Makes things more interesting."

My gaze lowers to the puzzle pieces inking his skin. "Then I'm curious what design you would implement to take care of the problem."

He glances at his tattoos, then looks me in the eyes, a smirk on his face. "Only I know the design of my puzzles. That's why I'm still here and free, despite what you may hear on the news. You're using a pattern. *Her* pattern. Do you think she won't figure it out? And if she does, others can too."

As he grabs the electrode rods, a sense of dread spears my chest. "Wait… What the hell? I thought we'd come to an agreement."

"I'm giving you seven days to implement your plan. When time runs out, I'll find you." He taps the rods together. "Ready for round two?"

"I already agreed to your fucking terms—"

"Oh, this isn't for me," he says. "It's for your girl. I feel she's entitled to a little of your torture."

I laugh, I can't help it. He's absolutely fucking right. If he cooks my brain, it wouldn't come close to atoning for what I've done to her. Yet, even if I can confess such a thing, doesn't change the fact I'd do it all over again just for a chance to make her love me.

"Mouthguard," I say.

Grayson smirks down at me. "You're earning another measure of my respect, Chambers."

As electricity courses my body, I watch the dim light of the floor lamp flicker along the ceiling as juice is sucked away. I count the seconds. I count until the induced seizures misshape the form of numbers in my mind's eye.

I lose consciousness.

When the torment's over, I pry my eyes open. My

eyelids feel weighted down. Like coming up quickly from the depths of the ocean, my body attempts to equilibrate. Nausea grips my stomach with acute urgency to vomit.

I turn my head and lean over the gurney. A bucket has been placed below.

Too drowsy and discombobulated to think of freeing myself completely, I flop back onto the bed and wait until I'm able to string a coherent sentence together without slurring my speech.

At the sound of his footfalls, I say, "I'm a little insulted you didn't create one of your elaborate traps for me."

Grayson swipes the scalpel from the table. "Not everyone can be special."

I blink slowly. My body is a languid puddle of soggy bones. I guess I should consider him gracious since he didn't crank the voltage higher than two hundred. I'll be sore, my muscles bruised, my brain sluggish, but I'll recover in less than twenty-four hours.

"Just remember the time, Chambers. I made it easy for you to keep track of." He uses the scalpel to cut the leather cuff away from my ankle. Then he slices through my pant leg.

For the first time, as I try to move my leg, I notice the tender soreness of my calf. Grayson lays the scalpel in my open palm. My fingers curl around the cool steel.

"I made a few alterations while you were out," he

says. "I think you'll appreciate the special detail I designed just for you."

Confusion wraps my head like a fuzzy blanket, one right out of the dryer, hot and crackling with static electricity. I grip the tool with weak muscles, the urgency to sit up battling with my body's desire to pass out.

As Grayson strolls toward the door, I meet his cool gaze. "Seven days isn't enough," I say.

Halted at the door, he looks around my bare lab, then he reaches into his pocket and produces a USB drive. *My* USB drive. The only memory chip with the recorded compound to my procedure.

"You have two weeks," he concedes. "But I'm taking this—" he waves the drive "—as insurance. When you deliver, I'll deliver."

"And if I don't?"

His features remain impassive. "I'll eviscerate you and feed your entrails to my pet fish."

I let him have the last word. As he disappears from the room, I hastily use the scalpel to cut through the restraints. Once I'm free, I glance around to make sure I'm still alone, then close my eyes briefly to brace myself. I tear my pant leg the rest of the way up the seam so I can inspect my leg, and sickness roils my stomach at the sight.

"Jesus Christ—"

The ticking I heard was not inside my head; it

wasn't some subconscious, delusional manifestation. It was fucking real. He had a pocket watch on him. He brought it here, knowing the whole damn time how this was going to end.

A clock face from an antique Rolex pocket watch has been stitched to the meatiest portion of my calf.

A goddamn watch is sewn into my leg.

After the initial shock wears off, I inspect further. Looks like he used 30 gauge, fine silver wire. Despite my resentment, I can appreciate the detail. The Rolex is a classic. The thin, pure silver chain of the watch has been wrapped around the timepiece and soldered to the watch casing, creating a pattern to which he used to stitch the wires through the chain links.

Sullivan was a welder in his previous life, I reason, as I cautiously touch the Rolex. My calf flames as I apply the slightest pressure, and the vibration of the ticking secondhand plucks my nerves.

That sick fucking bastard.

6

OUT OF THE SHADOWS

BLAKELY

Sweat trickles down the side of my face. I use the back of my gloved hand to wipe damp hair from my forehead before I bring my fists up and jab the punching bag.

I wrapped my hands with gel gloves, the same kind MMA fighters use. They work better for Jiu-jitsu training. Plus, I won't be wearing boxing gloves when I come up against Alex. Best to get used to having little protection over my hands.

I've been coming to this gym for over six weeks. It's close to my loft, and is nearly vacant at this time in the afternoon. I always stay later than my trainer. My flight from San Francisco was seven hours with the layover in Atlanta, giving me plenty of time to think.

London believes Alex will find me—that it's not a matter of *if* but *when*.

I kick the bag, imagining Alex's groin, envisioning the moment he's standing in front of me and what I'll have to do to take him down. I can't hesitate. I made the mistake of underestimating him once, and he put a needle in my neck.

This time, when he appears in my life, I won't give him the chance.

I started martial arts as an answer to the question that plagued me, whether or not Alex was really gone. Then I began to enjoy acquiring the skill. Knowing I can arm and defend myself physically where I'm emotionally impaired is empowering.

I now understand why women take self-defense classes.

There's some news program playing on the wall-mounted televisions, the prompt scrolling across the bottom of the screens warning an urgent message about the rise in fuel costs.

I have no idea what's going on in the larger world. It used to be a part of my job to keep up with current events, to talk intelligently with my clients and targets, to know how inflating costs would affect each job.

Now, I purposely avoid the news. I don't like the way all the grisly stories and tragedy makes me feel. I'm constantly fighting my own inner turmoil to keep my fluctuating emotions in check. I don't need outside sources influencing me there.

I adjust my ear pods and crank the music. Such a strange phenomenon lately, where I actually listen to music while doing tasks and training. I never comprehended it before. But as my heart flutters in my chest, and my head buzzes with the surge of adrenaline, I get lost in the sensation.

My fist sticks the punching bag hard, and the bag wobbles sideways. I catch it and start my routine again, my mind grasping at any distraction to prevent the one thought that only allowed me a few hours of sleep.

Having my suspicions confirmed brought on the nightmare, but this time, the faces of my revenge targets made cameos.

I take aim on the bag and lose myself for half an hour of intense focus. My wrapped knuckles take a beating as I visualize Alex's face as the bag. I see the moment so clearly in the dark forest, when I tried to escape and he blocked me with surprisingly skilled Jiu-jitsu moves. The shock I felt at his betrayal.

Not just the overall betrayal of the abduction and invasion of my person—but the duplicity, the expert way in which he masked his life into the ultimate lie to mislead me.

I groan and hit the bag harder, working out my aggression, which I never seem to work all out. It feels like a constant, irritating itch beneath my skin. As I land a fast strike to the bag, the music mutes as my phone dings with a notification.

I hold the bag, pulling in labored breaths to steady my heart rate. I remove an earbud and glance over at my tote. My phone lights up with an alert. I slip off my gloves and remove my ear pods before I swipe the notification open.

A prickle of dread touches the back of my neck. I recognize the name on the alert: Reilly Stafford.

Reilly was one of my first jobs. He was a really bad guy who more than deserved the revenge I doled out to him on behalf of my client.

Now he's dead.

His body was discovered behind a liquor store. Wallet and money missing. No shoes.

Twelve stab wounds to the torso.

A frantic laugh slips past my lips. I mutter a curse and rip the tape off my hands.

With most of my attention given to confirming Alex was even alive, I didn't stop to process the fact that he'd make the connection between me and Ericson's murder.

Or what it could mean if he figured it out.

Alex is no longer hiding. He's calling me out. He wants me to know it's him picking off my targets. Every single one has had the same MO as Ericson's murder; it's a blatant message right to me—his twisted way of telling me he knows.

So what is this to him…foreplay?

Some kind of warped hide-and-seek kink?

I drop down on the bench and shove my fingers into my hair, elbows pressed to my knees. I stare at the tiled floor, gaze unseeing.

Before, I rarely had doubts. No, I *never* had doubts. I always knew what my marks were thinking and how to access them. Hell, I've stalked stalkers before and set sophisticated traps for their revenge.

I want to believe I can read Alex, that I've come to understand his sick, demented brain—but the truth is, my rampaging emotions make me second-guess him, us…everything.

He was always unhinged. But he had a purpose. His belief system—no matter how flawed—kept him from losing complete touch with reality. I could always see a grain of sanity in his eyes even as he struggled with what he believed and his moral compass.

But what purpose does he have now? Why is he doing this?

And then I decide I don't care.

Trying to unravel the workings of a madman's brain is a descent right into madness itself.

All I know for sure is Alex is making a scene and drawing attention. He's not even hiding the bodies. He wants me to know.

But I'm not the only one who can draw comparisons.

A string of murders of wealthy financial advisors and rich pricks with the same methodology denotes a possible connection. It's a giant red flag—one that will damn sure be investigated.

I don't want the authorities to catch Alex.

He's mine.

I can't wait for him to come to me.

I push off the seat and grab my bag, heading to the locker room to shower and change. I strip my clothes and stand under the lukewarm spray, telling myself I'll get used to showering in a facility.

With three of my previous targets murdered, the detectives might even have already declared it a serial killer case. That will bring on more heat. Eventually, they'll narrow their scope enough that one of my identities will pop up on their radar.

Someone will come asking questions.

I constantly ask myself what Blakely would do. I need her fearless mentality right now, that clear-headed focus that cuts right through all the emotional bullshit to find the answer.

I turn off the shower and towel down, knowing that, even if there was a way to stall, I just don't have any more time.

The longer I have these feelings, the longer they sync with my mind and personality. I'm no scientist, but somehow I figure time will only make it harder to reverse the damage.

It might even be too late now.

Regardless, I have to try. There was a moment, one single instant where I thought Alex could see reason. He let me go. He burned his experiment to ash. He admitted his guilt over the lives he'd taken.

There was a moment in that dark room when sanity shown through.

I don't know what's happened to him since, but an unhinged person doesn't strategize and execute a plan of this capability. Either his actions back at the cabin were a part of a larger scheme, or something inside him has changed.

As soon as the thought strikes, I breathe a curse. I've been so obsessed with finding him, with correcting my own brain, that I didn't even think of him making the connection between Ericson's murder and his treatment.

Back at Devil's Peak, I convinced Alex that he had failed—that I was still the same unfeeling psychopath he'd brought to that cabin in the woods. His failure, coupled with my rejection, sent him over the edge. At least, that's how I took his clock-smashing, cabin fire meltdown.

Maybe he truly wanted to set me free. To let me believe he died in the fire.

Until the news of Ericson's murder hit.

What I didn't count on was his deduction that—with that fucking scientist brain of his—the reason why it had happened in the first place.

It wasn't an accident. It wasn't self-defense.

A heightened moment of uncontrollable emotion took hold of me, and the only outlet was to put a switchblade into the vile bully in an alley.

An action taken in the heat of the moment.

Psychopaths don't commit crimes of passion.

I leave the studio with a new trepidation chasing me through the city.

London was wrong. Alex won't find me; he's already *found* me. He's been watching me this whole time, studying me, analyzing his subject.

Every time I felt eyes on me and questioned my sanity, he was there.

He's been trying to recreate the outcome and prove it was a success by subjecting the highest profile psychopaths on my revenge roster to the procedure.

He's been so close to me this entire time.

And he's been leaving bodies in his wake. He's been failing. He can't replicate his outcome with me.

If I want him to show himself, I have to force him out of the shadows.

I have to threaten the one thing he desires the most. His successful subject. His proof the treatment worked.

Me.

7

PHYSICS

BLAKELY

I wonder if this is how Alex found me.

Did he first build a database of psychopaths and narrow his selection pool by parameters like physical attributes, difficulty of abduction, fuck-ability? Did he stalk me for days or weeks before he followed me to that night club with a whole plan already in place?

Or was it all random chance that we happened to be there at the same time, some twisted fate of the dark irony gods?

Seated on a metal bench, I pull my bucket hat down low over my eyes as I stare at my phone, glancing up periodically to watch the building across the street. I've stalked this spot before. When I accepted the revenge job for Addisyn Meyer, this is where I started, outside a pizzeria across from her townhouse.

The scent of fresh dough and marinara packs the air, transporting me back two years ago to when I was a woman who targeted strangers. For money. For thrill.

To keep Alex in the dark, I never returned to my loft. After the incident with Ericson, I was already off the grid, using a burner phone and avoiding Wi-Fi. I've been laying low since then, only paying with cash, so it wasn't difficult to find a cheap hotel and hole up for a couple days.

Then I started devising a strategy to find him.

What I know: Alex is targeting my revenge marks. What I can assume: if he's working down my list, selecting psychopaths with the highest tally, the ones I rated most deserving of revenge, then it's a logical leap he'll want Addisyn.

Initially, I thought Alex would skip this name on the list considering she's a woman. But then, he had no reservations about abducting and torturing me, did he? Some ashamed and obviously twisted part of me might even be jealous at the thought of him with her. Which is insane. It's hard to follow your instinct when that instinct is muddled.

Taking charge and getting into the mindset of the woman I once was, I got updates on Addisyn's whereabouts. Her job. Her love interests and friends (or lack thereof). Her family. I slipped into my old skin and tried it out, made alterations, and began watching her, waiting for the moment Alex might show his face.

Really, it's difficult to stalk two people at once.

You're constantly distracted, anxious, aware of everyone around you, and everything feels suspicious. Because, while I'm trying to catch Alex stalking Addisyn, there's the chance he'll catch me.

But then something curious happened over the past forty-eight hours. After I immersed myself in a familiar routine, pretending to be my old self sparked a hunger for the chase. Instead of fearing the adrenaline, dreading any heightened emotions that might be triggered, I let the rush consume and guide me.

Before, I skirted a dangerous line in order to penetrate my unfeeling shell.

Now, I feel everything.

The nervous flutter of my heart when I get too close to the mark. The euphoric buzz when I discover a detail they try to keep hidden. Even the anxious desperation to complete the job.

If I'm being honest, it's tantalizing…and addictive.

I could never understand why people took such reckless chances only to get caught. Like most of my clients, their husbands slept with a coworker knowing they'd likely be discovered, risking their marriage and careers.

I'm beginning to relate on a level that was

impossible before. I can even fathom why people cheat —why they're drawn to the danger. Why they seek it out, repeatedly, despite the threat of ruining their life.

I can even comprehend why Addisyn Meyer is the way she is. Why, two years ago, she fucked-over her best friend by literally fucking that friend's fiancé. Oh, this wasn't Addisyn's only affront, or else she wouldn't have made it to a top placement on my list. That sin just happened to be the tipping point for Mia, my client at the time, who sought me out after suffering Addisyn's abuse since high school.

Addisyn was a serial stealer. All women know the type. At least, most of my women clients had a "friend" like this, or knew a woman they worked with that fit the profile.

As a narcissistic psychopath, one that viewed herself as the center of the universe and coveted everyone's success as her own, Addisyn was a terror. Attractive, yes, but she weaponized her looks, targeting and preying on powerful men.

She tore families apart. Destroyed careers. She was a homewrecker from hell.

And she fed off of the lives she ruined.

She gets off on inflicting pain. Not so much physical suffering; she prefers the psychological variety. She craves breaking people mentally, leaving them hopeless. Only when her victim is absolutely wrecked, is she satisfied enough to move on.

· · ·

But she had a special place for Mia in her rotten heart. Whatever Mia had, Addisyn wanted for herself. She was so good at her manipulation, gaslighting her friend for years, making her believe the ridiculous lie of: "Well, aren't you happy I showed you who he really was before you married him?"

Sounds ridiculous, even to me back then. I didn't understand how anyone could fall for such blatant bullshit. But…feelings, emotions. Those damn complicated matters of the heart that refuse to allow us to listen to our brain.

No one wants to believe the people in their lives are truly malicious.

That was my client, until Addisyn took the game too far, and Mia's distraught, cheating ex-fiancé took his own life over the sordid affair.

For Mia, hurt turned into pain, and pain became anger. Anger mutated into seething hatred.

By the time she hired me, she wanted Addisyn disfigured.

Of course, back then, I had firm rules in place that stated *no killing* or *maiming*. So we agreed on the next best punishment for a narcissist like Addisyn.

Across the street, the townhouse door opens, and I watch my mark exit the building.

I wait for her to reach the crosswalk, taking

inventory of every shop window, corner and alley where a stalker could emerge, before I pick up my coffee cup and start trailing Addisyn.

I keep my distance, staying almost a block behind her as she navigates the sidewalk toward her destination. She used to have a high-paying career as an interior decorator. One of the avenues she used to hunt and seduce married men. After I demolished her reputation with a well-tailored revenge scheme, she now lives a low-key life as an assistant at a dog kennel.

Not physically disfigured as my client had wanted, but a disfigured life can be just as effective. When Addisyn's name is Googled, a swath of websites pop up. Every time a background check is run on her, a fabricated report is delivered of the gritty details of the lives she's ruined. An in-depth catalog of the people on her personal hit-list. The medical report of her extensive list of sexually transmitted diseases. Instead of felonies and misdemeanors, I created a report tailored to Addisyn, a disturbing and uncomfortable read for any employer, colored with vibrant images of her in various compromising positions—the very images she kept on her phone to blackmail her victims.

And for the cherry on top, I programed a bot that, no matter how many times she pays to have the information removed, or changes her name, is coded to her social security number.

It's hard enough for her to get a decent job, but in

today's society, where everyone lives online, Addisyn finds it near impossible to even get a date, never mind seduce anyone's man.

Maybe one day she'll opt to change her identity altogether, but for now, she's accepted her humble place in this world as a troll.

As I reflect inward, trying to analyze my feelings for Addisyn and what I did to her, I wonder if I should have some remorse for taking the revenge scheme to the extreme and never giving her a chance at redemption. But all I feel is satisfaction that, even two years later, she's still paying her dues.

I made sure to cover my tracks, making it difficult for anyone to link me to her profiles and background reports—but there's always someone better. And if she winds up murdered, she'll become part of an investigation that could potentially lead right to me.

Which is another reason why I chose to stalk Addisyn in the hopes of finding Alex. He can't take it that far. I'll pay the price for Ericson when the time comes, but I won't go down for Alex's crimes also.

I spend most of the day reading a thriller on my phone, hopping from coffee shops to bars, while keeping tabs on Addisyn's menial life. After two full days of this, I'm becoming agitated and nervous that I chose the wrong mark.

Where the hell are you, Alex?

It's this frustration and doubt that almost makes me

abandon Addisyn. But as I follow her toward a dance club, I decide a few drinks to soothe the burn isn't the worst idea. Then I'll start fresh. Move on to the next target on the list.

I dress in a black tank top and jeans, low profile but able to blend. I keep my small crossbody bag hooked around my shoulder rather than checking it. I lose the hat and decide to wear my hair in loose waves, obstructing part of my face. But really, in a dark and lively atmosphere like a club, where most patrons are inebriated, no one looks too closely at facial details.

With this in mind, I have a drink in my hand at all times, sipping slowly. I want the warm, comforting buzz to dull the sharp edge of tension, but I need to stay alert.

I turn down a few offers to dance. I'm not here seeking the distraction of sex. I haven't had sex since that night on the waterfall cliff with Alex, and the thought of being intimate with another person feels…wrong.

Rationally, I've been avoiding the physical act out of fear of feeling those same heightened and torn emotions. Scared of losing myself to the deep end. Terrified they're tied only to Alex and what that could mean—a connection that belongs only to him.

A wisp of fury curls within my veins.

How am I supposed to understand myself and what I actually feel if I don't test the theory?

I can't isolate myself forever. And I can't live in fear of my feelings for Alex.

I toss back the rest of my cocktail and leave Addisyn gyrating with some loser near the bar. I do a quick scan of the men within the vicinity, and I walk up to one with a cute smile and nice build.

"You'll do," I say, as I grab his flashy button-down and tug him onto the dance floor.

He doesn't protest as I turn my back to him and press up against his body, swiveling my hips erotically as a haze of club smoke mists the air around us.

I force his hands on my hips and thrust my ass into his groin, allowing the heated shot of alcohol to fuel my actions.

Don't think. Not about Alex. The experiment. Fucking *feelings*.

Nothing.

Impulse and carnal need only.

Bag pushed to my hip, I raise my hands and let them drape his shoulders as I move and undulate to the rhythm. I used to enjoy dancing. I still do, I find. Maybe even more so. The music is a living force as it careens through my system like an electric charge. I feel every intense beat, piercing octave, moving lyric.

The act of seduction is empowering. I was good at it; I had studied what men and women wanted, and I knew how to lure them in. I turn to face my dance partner, ignoring the smug smile on his face, and instead focus on my pleasure.

Somewhere inside me pulses a dull ache of doubt— a truth felt at my core that this isn't what I want, that it doesn't compare to what I've experienced. But I close my eyes and embrace the crescendo, focusing on the euphoric stream flowing through my body. I throw my head back as I'm swept away in the sensation.

He sweeps his hand over my ass, and I try not to recoil. I grip his shirt and rotate my body provocatively, holding on tight as if I have no choice, like it's my fucking salvation.

I feel the press of a warm body from behind. Ignoring the impulse to look, to push away, I stay in the moment. Strong hands seize my waist, and a charged current arcs over my skin. I allow myself to lean back into the stranger as his hand trails my hip purposefully and slips between my thighs.

I'm fire and brimstone, searing around the edges. The hazy smoke creates a canopy above, cocooning us and fusing our bodies together. I'm coming undone at the feel of his fingers curling into my shirt to grip me closer.

If I don't act now, I might lose my nerve. I open my eyes and latch on to the guy in front of me. "Kiss me," I demand.

His dark brows knit together in a confused expression, and I realize he can't hear me over the music. Before I'm able to act on my impulse, a hand collars my neck—the guy at my back. His fingers slide along my jaw and force my face sideways. Then I feel the brush of his mouth against my ear.

The scent of sandalwood and aquatic cologne spikes my adrenals, triggering a visceral reaction.

My body stills. My heart constricts in my chest to the point of pain.

"I missed you, my goddess, my Peitho," he whispers, his breath teasing the shell of my ear. "Don't make a scene."

His arm fastens around my waist, caging me in, anticipating my response to flee. "She was a force," I say, reiterating a point I've made before. "Not a goddess."

The guy in front takes the hint that I'm no longer interested and coasts away, taking up the backside of another woman. Leaving Alex and me alone in a haze of smoke and tension.

The strobe lights slow to the tender beat of the house music as it dulls into a quiet roar inside my head.

"It was torment staying away from you," Alex says.

His voice is a ghostly whisper from the grave. My nightmares and fantasies colliding. I close my eyes, my skin aflame. A riot of emotions war within me, and all I can do is sway within his arms.

I was right…and so was London.

I hunted him to this place, and he found me.

"What is it about night clubs that makes you unable to resist me?" I ask.

He nuzzles his face in my hair affectionately, pushing the strands aside and placing a delicate kiss behind my ear. "No one can resist you, Blakely. But I'll be damned if I stand back and watch another man touch what's mine."

I clasp my hand over his on my belly, my nails digging into his skin. He doesn't react. Instead, he tightens his hold and leads us away from the crush of bodies, guiding me off the dance floor toward a more secluded section of the club.

Panic flares in my veins, roiling my blood into a frenzy. Logic battles to the surface of my chaotic thoughts as I try to remember my plan.

More than any torture Alex has subjected on me, I hate the weak and unsure person he's reduced me to.

So I let him take me. I press against him and feel every inch of his body. I drag my hands over his arms and chest, his hips and thighs, searching for any weapons or syringes. As I move up his body, he grips my biceps.

He levels me with those killer blue eyes. His intense gaze sinks right through my skin. "I didn't come here to hurt you," he says, seeing through my seductive full body search.

I arch an eyebrow. "Just making sure you're not *carrying*," I say mockingly, reminding him of the time he tried to sneak a knife into an MMA fight. My gaze shifts to the bandage around his hand.

He notices my interest. "Consequences of touching the fire." His tone conveys a double entendre, but all I hear is he's wounded. He has a disadvantage.

He maneuvers us to the side of the DJ booth where he presses my back to a wall. He flattens his palm above my head, his body leaned into mine, as if we're merely having an engrossing conversation.

I let my gaze drift over him, examining him thoroughly. He's dressed down with jeans and a gray long-sleeved button-up. He practically fades into the background of the city's muted industrial tones. Alex has always known how to blend well.

His hair is longer. Unkempt and falling below his ears. I hate that I find it sexy. His build has changed some; more definition, toned, as if he's been working out just as hard as I have in preparation for this reunion.

He lifts his bandaged hand to my face, his fingers stalling before making a connection, then he touches the strands of a loose wave. "I'm glad you kept it blond," he says.

"What are we playing at, Alex?" I jump to the fucking chase.

"No games between us." He caresses the strand of hair admiringly. "Just the meeting of bodies, both exerting equal force on the other, causing the exchange of momentum, of energy." He moves in closer to demonstrate his point. "In the simplest of terms, a collision."

I believe him. From the very first moment we met, we crashed right into each other.

"It's physics," he continues. "And you're the only body I want to collide against. You're a force, my force. The personification of power and raw energy."

I hold his penetrating gaze as the club vibrates around us. "You destroyed your goddess, Alex," I say, giving in to his delusion. "You killed the very essence of her soul. You broke her. Now you need to repair her."

I should feel foolish talking in riddles, but with Alex, I have to get on his plane, I have to reach him. I'm either going to convince him to reverse the procedure, trusting that he won't cause more damage....because what choice do I have?

I either let him potentially fry my brain, or live trapped in this hell forever.

And I simply can't do that. One way or the other, this will end.

"No, you're perfect," he says, fingers trailing my neck. "You bleed now, you feel the wound. Every achingly beautiful emotion, you embody it. You're so much more than a goddess, you're what the goddesses envy."

I'm breathless for a suspended moment as his intensity holds me captive, then I shake myself from the daze. Impatience curls my hands into fists at my sides as I restrain the desire to make him bleed.

I should feel vindicated. He's confirmed at least one suspicion; he's been stalking me. He's seen me struggle, at war with who I'm becoming. But I don't feel anything but a blistering anger and the overwhelming desire to cause him pain.

His thumb feathers my bottom lip, and a dark hunger burns behind his eyes.

I turn my head away. "So what you're saying is, you have no idea how to reverse the procedure." I laugh mockingly, knowing it will wound his ego. "What kind of scientist doesn't know how to reverse his own treatment?"

He clasps my jaw and forces my face toward his, fingers bruising. "I know what you're doing. That tired logic won't work. Even if there was any way to reverse the process, I'd never do it."

I lick my lips and smile. "You know what I swore. Your procedure didn't corrupt the part of my brain that craves revenge."

His mouth tips into devilish grin, his hand slipping down to collar my throat, and I sense a level of predator in him I never encountered before. "We can fight," he says, "or we can fuck. It's your choice. You came looking for me. Personally, I prefer the latter, but I'm okay with anything that promises your hands on my body."

Apprehension threads my spine. This isn't the Alex I left in a burning cabin.

When I don't respond, he tightens his hold in warning, his touch igniting my blood like a lit match to kerosene. He moves in and gently places a kiss to my jaw, tracking his tongue over my skin. My body rebels and succumbs all at once, incapacitating me.

"Now that you have the ability, there are so many things I want to do to you, to make you feel." His heated words whisper along my skin.

My eyes close, as if I can shut him out, turn off the receptors. When he pulls away, I open my eyes, stoic. "You've changed," I say.

His features darken as he measures me coolly. "That's what love will do. You changed me, made me a different man."

Love.

That word is a weapon when he uses it.

Of all the poems and sonnets I've read, never once did I imagine the lovesick hero trying to destroy the object of his affection. I never understood what I read before, not deeply, not on an intuitive level.

But maybe those writers didn't see what I do when I look into Alex's eyes. Maybe there's some deeper level of love that goes beyond poems and sonnets, a darker love that is so maddening, you crave to destroy what you love only because you want it so badly, it has to be consumed or demolished.

It leaves you no other choice.

That love isn't the kind knights in shining armor lament about.

This is what it feels like to be loved by the villain.

"You've changed, too," he says, stroking his thumb down my chin reverently. "So I had to be better, to become more, for you."

I don't know what true love feels like, I have nothing to compare it to, or if anyone truly does, for that matter—but if this is love, then it's a vile sickness.

As he fixates on me, the club lights dim blue, shadowing his expression. My eyes are drawn to a patch of skin near his eye. My hand goes to his hairline, and I brush my fingers along his temple, feeling the rough scar. I push his hair aside to reveal the damaged skin. The wound is new.

My chest tightens, constricting the air in my lungs. I recognize the burn mark, because I have the same ones. I drop my hand as my mind goes to a dark place.

He captures my wrist and secures my hand between us. Then his gaze lingers on the scar along my temple. "Matching scars," he says. "We should get tattoos, too."

"Did you do that to yourself?" I ask, disgust evident in my voice.

A devious expression creases his eyes. "I was paid a visit by your friend Grayson," he says into my ear, his hand clenched around my wrist to the point of pain. "You know, right after you met with his psychologist."

A roar fills my ears, the music muted to a dull pulse. London.

Too many thoughts crowd my head, but one fights for dominance: I told London that Alex was a killer.

Alex regards my expression, his features losing some of the edge. "It's okay," he says, dipping his head to find my gaze. "I forgive you. It's my fault I wasn't there for you."

He's reading the wrong emotions in my mortified expression. I don't feel remorse; I'm petrified.

London deliberately lied to me. She knew, while sitting across from me and staring me in the eyes, that Grayson was already searching for Alex. She knew more than what I revealed to her, and...

"Do they know about Ericson?"

Alex doesn't take long to catch up to my train of thought. Suddenly the delusion fades from his eyes, and he stares at me with clear comprehension.

He leans in to say near my ear, "They know. But they don't know who killed him."

I take a moment to process this information before I look into Alex's face. Grayson subjected Alex to his own torturous treatment, just as London claimed he would. But he left Alex alive, an action not likely in a killer's nature.

And Alex found me. Now. Not because he was stalking one of my targets—but because he was searching for me.

Suddenly, I feel trapped.

I glance around the flashing club, wary of every set of eyes that look our way.

London could've subdued me. Grayson could've killed Alex.

They didn't.

They want something.

And Alex is here to deliver it to them.

Raising my hands slowly, I link my arms around Alex's neck. "We're making a scene," I say.

He's hesitant, his muscles stiff, frame locked and unyielding. I draw closer to him, aligning my body with his, every contour and curve fitted seamlessly. My breasts rub against his chest, the friction tightening my nipples, and I try to ignore the hollow ache between my thighs at the feel of his erection pressing against my pelvis.

There was never a question of whether or not Alex and I fit physically. His leanly carved muscular definition suits my physique. He's strong and can claim me on the side of a cliff, kiss me until I'm breathless under a waterfall—and it's so easy to close my eyes and fall into him.

He's familiar in a way no one else has ever been. Which makes it fucking confusing when my body is fighting need and my mind is battling with a heart that knows better, because he's already broken any chance of trust between us.

But this isn't about trust, or lust, or even love.

It's about staying alive long enough to know what comes next.

Despite my treacherous emotions, some facet of me wants to fight, to live. Maybe not in spite of but because of them. A toxic conundrum I don't have time to sort through right now.

I tip my head back and stare into Alex's vibrant eyes, lit by swirling lights and lust.

I feel the second his fight dissolves. His bandaged hand palms my lower back as his other goes to my nape, fingers splaying into my hair.

"Blakely…" His tone is urgent, my name a plea.

I wish that were enough.

If I had been born this way, maybe it would be.

"Fight or fuck, huh. Those are my options." I reach behind my back and latch on to his injured hand, digging my fingers into the bandage.

He recoils in shock, giving me enough time to grab hold of his shoulder and bring my knee up between his legs.

Only Alex catches my leg, slipping his hand beneath my knee and anchoring my body to his.

When his eyes meet mine, he smiles. "So predictable. Maybe you haven't changed all that much."

8

ENEMIES-TO-ENEMIES

ALEX

*L*ife is a gift. But not in the way most assume, like it's this miraculous chance to exist. That's missing the most obvious point, which is *not knowing* what came before life or what's to come after.

We started existing right in the middle—the present all we have to experience.

The absence of memory, that is the true gift.

Memory is filled with pain.

When you realize every day is a chance to be free of that misery, then you can truly start to live.

Otherwise, that debilitating past anchors us there, prevents us from taking leaps. That's why we can feel lost, wandering pointlessly, uselessly, waiting for something to happen—for life to finally *start*.

It already happened. You're *here*. That was your start.

When Grayson let me walk out of the condemned apartment, in essence, I was given a second start.

Not because he spared my life. Or because I have some new lease on my existence.

That fleeting bullshit doesn't impact me or my choices, which were already so ingrained with the woman I'm obsessed with. Because of her, I already shed that layer of guilt; my only misery weighing on me is the absence of her.

Even when the prolific Angel of Maine was holding the rods to my temples with the threat of cooking my brain, all I could think about was Blakely.

How we don't yet know how the changes will affect her long-term. How I need to be there for her, to help her adjust, to grow and evolve.

How she needs me to protect her.

A pure moment of clarity to sweep away any fears and doubts and spotlight my whole reason for existing.

Her.

She's more than just the answer to my question—she's my purpose.

Grayson had already taken away one woman from my life; I would be damned if I allowed him to take another.

The thought of damning my soul brings a slow, mocking curl to my lips. If there is such a realm as hell, then the devil is already welcoming me with open arms.

I have no soul to lose.

Or to sell, for that matter, but that didn't stop me from making a trade with the fiend himself for more time. A bargain with my own personal devil. What choice did I have? Go after Grayson with blinding fury and fight to the death? Reap vengeance on my sister's behalf? To what end?

Even if I thought slitting his throat with a scalpel would solve my problem, that grudge feels more like a distant memory than a need to sate. Too much has happened, too much has changed since Mary's death, and my initial reason for the project has altered beyond that of a cure.

The most amazing scientific discoveries are sometimes by accident, a random chance.

A beautiful new start.

Like Blakely and I now, dancing to a tune of our own, tangled in a web of violence and blazing heat.

The gift of life started with an explosion, a literal bang amid the void, where all that is passion and chaos was born.

This moment here, this is our big bang.

We were created in a fiery collision, and if she needs to fight and draw blood within the chaos, then I'll suffer her wrath, because I know the beauty that awaits us when our system aligns.

Hand fixed to the soft pocket of her knee, I draw her leg around my hip, fusing us together so she's unable to attempt another attack. Truthfully, I'm not surprised or even hurt by her intended manipulation. I'm surprised she hasn't Tasered me yet.

"I thought confiding my torture in you might gain me a degree of sympathy," I say as I shove her back to the wall. She fits against me perfectly. We were designed for each other.

"I feel absolutely nothing for you." Pure disdain masks her beautiful features. "No, that's not true. Thanks to you, I know what unadulterated hatred feels like."

The malice lacing her words sends a heated charge over my skin. I've missed her mouth, her touch, even the vitriol she carries in her gaze. Feeling the press of her body to mine is making it damn hard not to touch her, to taste her everywhere.

I thrust between her thighs, my entire body searing to feel her skin against mine. "You can lie pretty well now, too," I say, grinding the shaft of my rock-hard cock along her heat. "But I can still read the truth in your body."

Her hand flattens against my chest, her expression creased in a mixture of agony and yearning. "Can you read a fucking slap to the face?"

I don't stop her. From this close proximity, the angle is awkward and it's not a strong slap, but she backs it with enough force to leave a lingering sting.

I never drop her gaze. Her chest heaves, her emotions cresting right along with her cleavage over the top of her shirt. She's the epitome of sin and temptation; my muse I can't resist.

"God, you're not even human anymore," she says.

The lights, the smoke, the scent of her skin—it affects all five senses to create a violent storm within me. *Human.* No, she altered me, and I'm no longer just a man. Some beast has taken up residency and is gnashing from the inside to get out and claim her.

We're locked in this battle together, her eyes searing me, my desire to never let her go dominating my willpower. The music is a fucking aphrodisiac coaxing me like a siren's song to taste her lips.

She seems to sense my urgency, and a sprig of panic blooms behind her eyes. "You're losing your mark," she says, nodding toward the dance floor. "Addisyn is leaving the club."

I don't even look. "I'm not here for Addisyn."

She doesn't appear surprised. She's smart enough to have already put it together. To find her, I took Grayson's insight and reversed the stalking process. He found me by using Blakely's list. I had to assume he was right, and that Blakely would also start watching her previous targets.

Since Grayson left me with little time and a literal ticking warning adhered to my body, I didn't have time to waste. I've been watching two of her targets.

"Right," she says. "And here I was almost jealous, since I thought I was the only woman you tortured. But I guess she's not an ideal candidate for your new murder project."

The way her eyes spear me, the judgement…she thinks she has me all figured out. She has no idea what we're up against.

"The truth is far more disconcerting," I say.

"If you don't release me, I *will* make a scene. I swear, Alex."

I hold her a moment longer, weighing the cost of her kiss, and decide night clubs have never worked in our favor.

Without verbal acknowledgement, I release her but only to take hold of her hand. Then I head toward the stairs that lead to a closed-off section connecting two buildings. While she was dancing, letting another man grope her, I was scoping out the building to mark all exits and blind spots.

She doesn't fight me, not yet. She wants privacy as much as I do.

I remove the chain barring access to a door I broke the lock on earlier. I shove the metal door open to the building skywalk, then drag her into the secluded bathroom. The bass of club music echos around the narrow space. My ears ring, the sounds distorted and muted as my hearing strains to adapt.

Her hand slips from mine, and I turn to face her. Under the wavering florescent lights, she's even more beautiful. Hair wild from dancing, mascara smudged from sweat, her top clinging to her curves from the humidity.

Some emotion crosses her features but, even after all my documentation and analysis, sketching every expression, studying every nuance, I'm having difficulty deciphering it.

She wets her lips, and I'm reduced to a pathetic, envious wretch at watching her tongue travel over her mouth. "You set the fucking cabin on fire," she says.

I blink, my thoughts leaping frantically to gauge her meaning. "I was distraught," I answer. "The woman I loved rejected me."

"That's a tad bit melodramatic, don't you think?"

I chance a step toward her. "I sacrificed my life's work to set you free," I challenge.

"Then you started it right back up," she fires back, "in my backyard."

All retort dies on my tongue. Logically, I know this argument is useless. There's nothing I can say to convince her of my reasoning. I did abduct her. I did conduct mind-altering experiments on her against her will. I did torture her mentally, physically, and I did abandon her.

And then when she experienced a slim measure of stability, security, I stole it away by resuming the experiment. I never let her in on the inner workings, keeping her in a pitch-black chamber of unknowing.

I can empathize with this feeling of helplessness. I endured it every time I lost myself in my room of clocks. I never meant for Blakely to become trapped there. That's why I destroyed it.

"I am the villain," I say, daring another step closer to her. "But most villains have a good reason with good intensions for their madness. It just gets away from them."

Like scientifically proving to myself that Blakely harbors the capability to love.

"I'm narrow-minded when it comes to my work," I add. "I can only see the numbers, the data. I can only focus on the result...missing what's literally right in front of me."

She pushes her hands into her pockets, shoulders defensive. "I watched you die, Alex. I watched the cabin burn. You let me believe you burned to death in that fire."

I tilt my head, carefully assessing her micro expressions. The way her eyebrows draw together briefly, the way her nostrils flare, the hard, achy swallow that drags along the slender slope of her neck. Less than half a second as it flits across her features, but I recognize the emotion.

Remorse.

All my walls come crashing down. She was *sad* I was dead. She felt *sorrow*. Even if she refuses to acknowledge those feelings inside her, she can't disguise her subconscious, involuntary display.

She has no practice.

And I am an idiot. It never occurred to me how my death would affect Blakely. I was so focused on the outcome, duplicating the experiment, I failed to see the most obvious thing of all.

I reach out to her. "I didn't realize—"

She retreats away from me. She whips the leather bag over her head and drops it to the dingy floor. "Don't ever touch me again."

I ball my fingers into a fist and drop my hand. This will take time, I know this. But the sheer thought of time has my heart tripping faster.

"I didn't realize," I try again, structuring my statement to spare both our egos, "that the treatment had been successful until it was too late. I thought approaching you in your new life would be too distressful, would discourage your…acclimation. So I opted to recreate the result on a new subject to collect my data."

She makes a sound of contempt. "Subjects, Alex. Plural. My targets. From my client list and personal notes. People who are all *dead* now."

Agitation borders impatience. They're not worthy of

her coveted feelings—they're merely samples. I spear my fingers into my hair. "Yes, as always, I'm quite used to my failures."

She shakes her head. "That's all they are to you. That's all *I* am. A result."

"No, you're wrong." I want to tell her everything I feel for her, to remind her of the connection we shared at the fall, how I could try an infinite number of ways to quantify why she's different from any other subject—why she's different for me—how she changed the result, my purpose, and that's why I need empirical data and evidence.

Because without rational, sound reason, I'm a slave to my feelings for her. I have no control.

Out of desperation, I step toward her and grab her arm, momentarily forgetting Blakely's investment in martial arts.

Reflexes sharp, she spins out of my reach and removes her hands from her pockets, clutching some object. "I'm not leaving here until you tell me the truth about what you've done to me, and how you're going to fix it."

I wipe my hand over my mouth. "I told you, there is no way to reverse the treatment," I tell her honestly. "Once new neural pathways are created, they can't be closed. They're not a light switch I can toggle on and off. Not without permanent, necrotic damage to the cells."

In other words, death.

"What you underwent," I say, wishing I could translate numeric equations into words, "was extreme, for lack of a better explanation. Any further—"

"I understand," she cuts me off. She stares past me into the mirror, a faraway look slipping over her face. When she directs her attention my way, I glimpse an echo of her former self. "All I want is my life back, you insane shit. I want *myself* back. If you can't give me that, then we're done, Alex. It's over."

I see her muscles tense as she closes the distance. I see her right shoulder drop. I make a split-second decision not to block her attack and let Blakely punch my face.

The impact jars me for a suspended moment, delaying my reaction time. My jaw takes the brunt of the strike, whatever solid object she's holding distributing the impact without give.

She goes to deliver another punch, like she's compulsively practiced on that punching bag, and I capture her arm and shoulder in an arm-lock to restrain her movements. We grapple like this, her wriggling to loosen my hold, me refusing to take her down, until she forces me to sweep her leg. I catch her around her lower back before she hits the floor.

"Your emotions are hindering your decision making," I say.

"No fucking shit." She jabs my ribs. On reflex, I release her.

She lands on her ass, but recovers quickly, rolling onto her hip. She swipes her foot out and takes me down beside her.

A laugh bursts free. "You've gotten good with your training."

She groans as she gets to her knees. "I knew you were watching me, you sick—"

"Watching *over* you," I tell her, turning onto my side and raising my hands in time to block her fist. Her jab stings the hell out of my palm, and I circle her wrist, squeezing hard to make her open her hand.

A roll of nickels clatters to the tiled floor. "You're going to break your fingers. And I like your fingers."

She tries to jerk out of my hold, but I won't release her. "It was supposed to break your face."

I catch her other hand as it comes toward my stomach. I meet her sea-green eyes brewing with a storm. "And after you're done beating the hell out of me, what are you going to do? Where are you going to go? You need me, Blakely."

She narrows her gaze, rage brimming around the edges. "If you can't fix me, then there's absolutely nothing I need from you. Let me go."

"Never," I say. "I'm never letting you go again."

I might have been able to leave her once before. I could've even forced myself to stay away. But touching her now, breathing the same air as her, feeling her heart pound against my chest…

This is over for me.

I'd let Grayson eviscerate me with a dull butterknife if it meant keeping Blakely forever.

I give her the chance to make good on her threat and drop her wrists. She holds my gaze a second before she raises her arm and sends her elbow toward my nose. Since I can't have a broken nose added to my list of ailments to slow me down, I catch her fist and twist her arm downward, pinning her forearm behind her back and forcing her chest against mine.

Before she can strike with her left, I lock my hand around her arm and pin it to her thigh.

I look down into her face, wondering just how far her anger extends, if she's willing to sacrifice injuring herself to hurt me. One headbutt would free her.

"I don't mind doing this all night," I say, unable to suppress a smile. "But we do have urgent matters to discuss. Just let me know when you've had enough."

"Fuck you."

My dick jumps at the thought. I groan, so damn tempted.

A shot of anger ignites her eyes, and she cranes her head back.

Instead of letting her injure the both of us with a headbutt, I release her arms and grab the backs of her thighs. I pull her forward and drop her back to the floor.

Essentially, I've put her in the guard position which, had she trained more with grappling rather than punching, she'd realize she's in the most powerful position.

I push between her thighs. As she straddles me, I bear down on top of her, restraining her wrists above her head.

I stare down and admire how her heavy breaths strain her breasts against her top. After a few useless attempts to free herself, her fight wanes. She relaxes her muscles and rests her head on the floor.

"Why are you just staring at me, you freak."

"I'm trying to decide what I want to do more." I thrust hard against her, earning a soft moan from her lips. "Whether I want to tear your pants off and taste you, or shove my fingers deep inside—"

Her thighs crush my midsection in an attempt to remove me. When that fails, she rests again. "How was it so easy to kill a man by accident, yet I can't murder the one I want intentionally."

"Because, beneath all those raging emotions, you don't actually want to kill me. I'll let you in on a little secret about the emotionally capable." I secure her wrists in one hand so I can maneuver lower down her body. Using my teeth to drag the hem of her top up, I expose the soft skin and delicate curve of her abdomen that I've sketched from memory.

"Hatred and love, they're nearly indiscernible," I

say. "Passion rules us, and anger is felt at its height when either of those emotions take hold."

"You're beyond deranged if you believe we're in love."

I drop a kiss to her belly, parting my mouth to trail my tongue over her flesh, eliciting tiny ripples of gooseflesh and a breathy sigh from her lips. It's crazy inducing. I'm battling the frenzied urge to strip her naked and sink so deep inside her, she won't be able to deny our connection.

"We're not in love," I agree with her. "We're in need, in *pain*. Love is merely dopamine and norepinephrine, chemicals produced to dull the pain. Not for long, though. Because that pain? Pain is real. Pain to complete a connection and satisfy the need. It's sick and villainous and twists us, but we have to answer that demand."

Her hips flinch in response. She barely moves, but the slightest press of her pussy against my cock nearly decimates me.

"Christ, you're making me come undone, Blakely." I lie my forehead to her chest, intoxicated, drunk on her lure. I don't even care if she squeezes the life out of me. I'd welcome her pain and pleasure equally.

Everything about her is the same, but different. She's softer. Fragile and fearful. Strong, and even just as cunning, but she's questioning. She never hesitated before. She'd never allow me to hold her against the floor as she contemplated her move.

I'd be the one on the floor.

The woman who Tasered me and shot me up with club drugs is still present, but now there's a vulnerable undercurrent that begs to be touched.

And, oh, I want to touch that part of her greedily.

But the ticking in my head grows louder, sounding over the thump of music, reminding me she's in trouble.

That's why I'm here. That's why I'm giving up any progress and discovery and breaking my rules to be here with her right now and convince her she needs me.

With painful regret, I let go of her leg and separate from her. But before I release her completely, I palm the side of her face and tilt her head back. Her gaze is curious as she stares up at me, as if she's trying to piece together what I'm holding back.

Then, she says, "They want me dead."

I shake my head, staggered at how she came to the conclusion. "I assume Grayson and London want us both dead," I confess. "But first, they want us to get rid of any connection tying Grayson to the subjects."

"Victims," she says.

"I'm not delusional." I sink my fingers into her hair at the nape of her neck. Then I take what's right before me, what's been taunting me since the moment I laid eyes on her.

I slant my mouth over hers and kiss Blakely with the

hunger of a starved man. Delusional or not, when her lips crash against mine, I feel the alignment of our system, and I know she feels it, too.

As we move in sensual tandem, inhaling and exhaling each other, her tongue slips over mine and sends a wild craving coursing my veins. It's sheer bliss and torment, the burning desire only heightened, never extinguished.

Her teeth nip at my broken lip before she bites down into the kiss. The sharp pain webs through me like lightning cracking the sky, and I taste the metallic trace of blood. She tears free, her breaths ragged and eyes wild. Then her fist makes contact.

9

OURS IS MAD

BLAKELY

*P*ain explodes along my knuckles and radiates up my arm. My fingers feel smashed from the impact of my fist meeting Alex's cheek. But the hurt is so damn good, cathartic.

His face shifts sideways. He leaves his head in that position, letting the pain simmer as he licks blood from his bitten lip.

My lungs are on fire as I drag in a full, searing breath. The atmosphere of the bathroom starts to filter in with the muffled punch of bass from the club next door. The walls rattle, the dim fluorescents above flicker. As my senses slowly return, my mouth is hot and swollen, and I wipe the back of my hand across my aching lips.

A deviant part of me rises to the surface at the taste of Alex's blood in my mouth, igniting a hunger for more violence.

I pump my hand, working out the throb in my fingers. "That was satisfying."

Alex spits a red stream before leveling me with intense blue eyes. "We have different definitions of that word." He pushes to his feet and stares down at me. "Do you need to hit me again, or was that finally enough?"

"Not even close." My heart tears a wild path through my chest as I scramble to stand and pull back my fist to land another strike, all restraint shattered.

Every volatile emotion swirled into a chaotic vortex as his lips caressed mine, taking me to those dangerous, heightened cliffs where I fear losing control.

That can't happen.

I breathe through the rush. Adrenaline scorches my veins like flame to fuel. My skin is heated and stretched too tight, an itch digging beneath my flesh.

As I step into the swing, Alex doesn't allow me to get a hit in so easily this time. He expertly blocks my fist and slaps my forearm aside, leaving him a clear shot to my face.

He hesitates.

His eyes capture mine.

With a breathless curse, he moves in and grabs me around my waist. Arm banded around my back, he hitches my ass up onto the counter and forces his hips between my legs.

His cologne assaults my senses, that aquatic fragrance that reminds me of fresh river water. The warmth of his body heat touches every pulse point, making my nerves spark. I'm violent as I try to tear away from him, hating him, hating myself, for what's happening to my body.

"Get the fuck away—" I nail a fisted hand against his shoulder.

"You keep coming at me." He seizes my bruised hands and locks them between us. "Fuck, Blakely. I don't want to hurt you." His breath slices the air, those vibrant pale-blue eyes piercing me.

A manic laugh rises up from the base of my throat. "It's a little late for that. The damage is done." I shake my hair from my eyes, fixing him with a hard stare. "And now that you have a deranged killer threatening my life, I say there's nothing left to do but tear each other apart. At least I can get my revenge before Grayson turns me into some insane trap."

His features soften, understanding bleeding through the heated tension. "You forget who reached out to the psycho couple in the first place," he says, accusation clear in his tone. "What did you tell Dr. Noble? It had to be good to have her patient this interested in us."

Some of the fire within me dissipates. Obviously, what I told London made its way to Grayson. I didn't realize this was a risk, or consider the consequence of Alex and me having to face off against a vigilante. Not until after London left my hotel suite. I realized only too late the two of them might be involved.

"Everything that's happened after the moment you stuck a needle in my neck is on your head, Alex." Righteous fury slits my gaze. I hope my eyes flay him.

His features draw tight. "I'm going to fix this."

"You can't fix this. You can't even fix *me*. I killed a man," I say harshly under my breath. "My brain is wrong. I'm wrong." I shake my head, acceptance weakening my resolve.

His hands fall to my hips. "Tell me what happened."

My eyes close against the flash of memory. I haven't spoken in depth about that night to anyone, and Alex is the last person I want to confide in. But he's the cause; he did this to my brain. If there's a chance he can glean one vital peace of information that can undo what's been done…

So I tell him about my mission to complete the Ericson job. About following Ericson to his apartment building. The cry for help I heard in the alley, and how it affected me, forced me down that dark passageway.

"He was strangling her," I say, recalling the abuse I witnessed, how I feared Ericson would actually kill the woman. "And when her eyes met mine… I don't know. I don't remember all the details. One moment he came at me, then his back was turned." I take a staggering breath. "I reached into my bag, then I was stabbing him. Blood all over my hands."

I turn my face away, as if I can avoid the barrage of images assailing me. Alex touches my chin, gently coaxing my gaze on him. "It was self-defense, then."

I jerk my head out of his hold. "No. I know that much. Something fractured inside my head. The rage I felt, I'd never experienced anything like it before. I was out of control."

"And that terrified you the most," he says, and I hate the way his eyes brim with understanding.

I sniff back the burning threat of furious tears, a mocking laugh falls free. "Yes. I fucking hate not being in control of my thoughts, my emotions, my actions. What the fuck else am I capable of?"

His hands fist the slim give of my jeans along my hips, tugging me closer to him. Heat pools between my thighs where his body touches mine, and I fight the urge to wrap my legs around him.

I've seen all shades of Alex before. The gullible nerd. The intelligent scientist. The *insane* mad scientist. The smoldering man fighting carnal need. The remorseful sinner he became when faced with his demons.

But I've never seen the darkness pit out his eyes the way it is now, reminding me of his room of clocks, a hollow void of blackness.

"Alex, what?" I demand. "What aren't you telling me?"

"I've given you no reason to trust me," he says. At my impatient glare, he expels a breath. "The procedure didn't change you. It can't... Personality traits aren't altered, just magnified."

Cold trickles beneath my skin. "You're saying I'm a killer. That's just...who I am."

He takes hold of my face, a mix of desperation and determination carved in his features. "We both know Ericson was deserving of that punishment. He probably deserved worse."

Breath bated, I try not to move. "I wasn't his judge," I say, my voice devoid of conviction.

He drags his thumb across my bottom lip, eyes lit with raw hunger. "But you were his executioner," he says. "You once said revenge was your ethos. It still is, just...magnified."

Fear is a tidal wave crashing over me, pulling me so far below the surface I can't catch my breath.

"You're wrong. You're so fucked up and wrong." But even as I deny his words, my heart rate quickens, my pulse jumps in my veins. The numb cold is replaced with a rush of liquid fire to ignite my blood. A white-hot spike of adrenaline pours through me, almost intoxicating.

I experienced this very feeling while stalking

Addisyn. The rightness of it, the same rush I always felt at the start of a job, the initial stage of the hunt.

As I struggle to free myself from Alex, he forces my arms above my head and pins both wrists to the mirror. My lungs fight for oxygen, my chest rising to push against the solid wall of his chest.

The brain cells that capture memory fire in rapid response. I recall the taste of our first kiss. Our first touch. What it felt like as he entered me on the cliff of the waterfall. The assault is overpowering, confusing my fight or flight response.

My skin crackles where he touches. Everything in me wants to rip his eyes out and punch his smug mouth. But something primal squirms in my belly and lower, tempting me to arch against him, the desire for friction to offset the needy hunger too strong.

It's not just physical; it's the yearning for closeness. All those lonely, sleepless nights where I clung to his shirt with some foreign need to be comforted.

"If I'm wrong, then we're wrong. And I refuse to accept that," he whispers over my lips, his eyes smoldering embers. "Goddamn, you're all I think about, all I want."

His mouth descends on mine, stealing my breath and the last of my fight.

The kiss isn't soft and questioning; it's all take and blaze, desperately trying to sate a sinister need that wants to devour us.

I've wanted to believe what I felt at the waterfall was a glitch. Some crossed wires in my brain along with survival instincts triggered an extreme response. That there's no way in hell I could've been with Alex like that…felt all of those things for him any other way.

But just like a moment before, kissing Alex brings it all rushing back. My chest is on fire. The aching hunger to consume and be consumed too severe, and the pain borders on pleasure.

My body dissolves under the swell, strained muscles giving in as I'm being pulled under the current. His grip on my wrists loosens, and I link my arms around his neck as my mouth moves in time against his. My heart thunders as his tongue expertly sweeps inside the hollow of my mouth to tangle with mine.

I'm achy and starved and furious. Every emotion on the red spectrum burns through me as I fist my fingers in his hair, a desperate sound emanating from deep in my throat.

Alex groans as his hand collars my throat, holding me in place against the mirror. Fear only serves to heighten the arousal, and I know it's wrong, only I can't shut off the flood of emotions. Painfully, he pulls away from the kiss. His thumb rests heavily against my pulse as his gaze tracks my distressed features.

He removes one hand from my waist to gently touch my temple. He traces the scar, the one he put there from the electrodes when he shocked me with more voltage than a person should sustain. "Our scars define us," he says, "inside and out."

He presses a kiss to the scar. A tender ache lodges in my throat and my sinuses flare, threatening to unleash a torrent of livid tears.

"There is no one else like you, Blakely. You're that rare. You'll never be able to live an ordinary life, simply because you're extraordinary. That kind of significance is isolating, but we don't have to be alone."

A serrated edge rises up between us, severing his mental hold. I lift my chin, swallowing against the pressure of his hand around my neck.

"I'm not alone," I say.

Alex moves in, but halts inches from my lips. A coy smile tugs at his mouth to make that infuriating dimple deepen in his cheek. "Why do you sleep with my shirt?"

My pulse trips. "To keep the fury burning."

"So much passion." His head shakes slightly. "Do you really want to be rid of it? That fire that lets you know you're alive?"

I steel my features. "I would tear it out with my bare hands if I could."

He feathers a finger down the side of my face, his hold around my neck cinching tighter. "You can fight it, even physically fight me, but you know what it feels like to make a deeper connection now. Even if it was possible, you can't go back to that numb state. You'll always crave me in your system."

"God, I fucking hate you."

"Show me how much you fucking hate me."

The dare hovers—charged and volatile—in the sliver of air separating us. Waiting for one of us to move, to submit, and topple the first domino. Letting every wall and barrier crash down.

Since the day I ran from the fire, I've been trying to escape a blaze of emotions. Make them stop. Bury them. Do anything other than *feel* them.

Sex is a drug, and like all drugs, it can deaden the pain. And all I want is one moment of relief.

I grab Alex's shirt and drag him forward. We collide in a blistering inferno of lust and loathing and pure, unadulterated need.

I dig my ankles into his backside as my fingers fumble his shirt open. "I hate your stupid glasses," I say, pulling away to tear his sleeves down his arms.

"I'm wearing contacts." He tosses the garment to the floor and yanks his white undershirt off.

"I hate your pretty blue eyes."

He fists the hem of my tank top and pulls it up over my head. "I love your stormy green gaze."

My hands slip over his shoulders, my blunt nails raking down his back, as Alex grabs my ass and hauls me off the counter. He kisses me until I'm breathless, then drops my feet to the floor and spins me around.

I latch on to the rounded edge of the basin, chest aching, the pulse of the music competing with the pounding thump of my heart. He slips his hands to the front of my jeans and works the clasp open, lowering the zipper too agonizingly slow.

I slam my eyes shut against our reflection. "Just fucking do it."

His movements stall. Then, with a fierce groan, he tugs the waist of my jeans down and spins me around, forcing my eyes on him.

Fire and ice clash in the depths of his eyes, an unhinged conflict of yearning and fury fighting for dominance.

Jaw clenched, he thrusts his hand down the front of my panties. His fingers rub over me with hot friction, and an ache pinches inside my core, buckling my knees. He spreads me open with two fingers, and I can sense how wet I am, how slick his fingers feel as he circles my clit before pushing inside me.

"Goddamn," he mutters on an uneven breath. "Punching me gets you this wet…"

A flame of humiliation licks over me, and I don't realize I've slapped him until my palm smarts with the sting. Alex licks his lip, gathering the fresh bead of blood, before he grabs the back of my neck with his bandaged hand and draws me closer.

I reach behind and grip the counter, arching my back as he furiously fucks me with his fingers. My nipples harden against the sheer material of my bralette, seeking the rough plane of his chest. The ache plunges deeper, snatching my breath, my hips undulating as I ride his hand shamelessly.

I rock my hips in desperate need to rub my clit against the heel of his hand, and Alex stops.

I open my eyes, my gaze meeting his through a haze of lust and crushing yearning that threatens to break me if he doesn't touch me again soon.

"Tell me to taste you," he says, his voice gravel with the harsh demand.

Breaths ragged, I match his intense stare. "No."

Before I lose my mind to him, I embrace the welling anger and shove his chest, breaking his connection. His effort to capture my arms is thwarted as I jab his wounded ribs. I shove his shoulder and push past, so close to escaping...until his arms circle my waist.

"I think you need the fight." He crushes my back to his chest.

I can't deny anything, unsure of my own feelings—these fucking excruciating emotions that beg me to surrender and fall into Alex, to just lose myself completely in the pleasure.

He picks my feet off the floor and carries me toward one of the stalls. With what fight I have left, I plant my foot to the cinderblock wall and kick off, smashing his back into the stall.

The hinges creak, and the flimsy divider gives a fraction. I struggle to free one of my hands and claw my nails down his forearm. He stumbles back harder into the stall. It splinters, cracking until the bolts *clink* to the tile.

"I'll tear the world down with you," he says, his heavy breaths an erotic sound at my ear, our chests rising together in sync. "If that's what it takes. Shatter for me, baby. I'll let you break against me."

A violent tremble takes hold of my body. I hate every word from his mouth. I hate the pressure building in my chest. I hate the ache that threatens to rip me in half.

"I hate you—"

Alex pushes away from the divider and releases me, but only to turn my back flat to the broken surface of the stall. His gaze is molten, a blazing blue that steals my breath.

"You can hate-fuck that pussy against my mouth until I suffocate," he says, his hands taking hold of my jeans. He shoves my jeans down, towing my panties with them, and drops to his knees.

My lungs threaten to burst as I breathe through the devastating sensation of his mouth surrounding me. My eyes fasten shut as I let him strip my shoes and pants off so he can bring my leg over his shoulder. He sucks my clit between his teeth, and I press my palms to the cool stall, needing to be grounded.

The arousing sensation of his stubble grazing the sensitive skin of my inner thighs sends me reeling, and I undulate my hips, begging for more friction.

Alex latches on to my thigh as he licks a hard seam up my slit. His tongue skillfully plunders between my lips as he works my clit harder, making me shiver. The yearning to crest is overwhelming, and the edges of fear bleed into euphoria. I'm so close to losing all control.

I tunnel my fingers into his hair, nails scraping his scalp, and grip hard. He groans against me, bringing on the first wave of the pending orgasm, and my core pulses with aching need.

I cry out and bring my knee up against his jaw.

Alex curses and staggers back, planting a hand behind him to break his fall. He stares up at me with gritted teeth and hot anger searing the edges of his restrained desire. The sight of smeared blood along his lip pulls at some base craving within me.

We go for each other at the same time.

His hands clasp around my waist as my nails sink into his bare shoulders. Our mouths collide, all savage, vicious want, and the coppery tang of blood bleeds into the kiss, turning it brutal, punishing.

He smashes my back against the stall, and the weak panel finally gives completely. Alex brings my chest against his and deftly swivels me on top of his body as the divider crashes into the next stall, then slides to the floor.

All my weight bears down on him, our bodies fused together, but we're too far gone to care about the wreckage around us. The need to tear through every barrier preventing us from touching, skin to skin, is shred in violent fury as he snaps my bra away and I work his jeans open.

We wrestle the rest of our clothing from our bodies while lashing into each other with intent to feel every kiss, bite, stroke, our hands and limbs tangling. As Alex kicks his pants down his legs, he breaks the kiss.

"Wait," he says, breaths torn, chest expanding with each vital intake.

"No. Take off your pants," I demand, the torturous idea of waiting any longer too painful. I can't allow my mind to have time to *think*.

"Blakely, wait—" The urgency in his voice breaks through the hazy lust between us, and I pull back slowly.

With eyes sealed tight, he says, "Grayson did something…"

The way he chokes on the last syllable, panic flares inside my chest. I lift up to glance down at his crotch, fearful a deranged serial killer severed a certain body part—but no. I *felt* him, hard and long and pressed into me.

Did he cut off his balls?

Searching his body, I finally see what Alex is referring to, and all I can say is: "Huh. That's…fitting."

He sighs heavily beneath me. "He gave me a literal countdown until he comes for us."

Tentatively, I reach behind me and run my fingers

over the inflamed skin. "Jesus." I carefully touch the wires fucking *stitched* into his flesh.

The glass face of an old pocket watch has been sewn into his calf. The secondhand jumps, counting down the minutes, and I can't help but to observe the time.

We've lost all track of it while we've been inside this room, closed off from the world. And I realize that's never happened before, not where Alex is concerned. Every moment at the cabin together, time was measured, recorded. Unescapable.

"I wasn't awake," he says, drawing my thoughts away from that dark place.

I face forward and stare down at him, planting my hands on his chest. "That's too bad," I say, lowering myself on top of him. "I was hoping you felt every painful stitch."

He reaches up and threads his fingers into my hair, holding the side of my face reverently. "No one is capable of making me feel pain like you, Blakely Vaughn. You own that power alone."

I take sadistic comfort in his confession.

As he holds my gaze, I move my hips, sliding over his cock painstakingly slow, drawing his thoughts away from clocks and time and threats.

A heavy sigh fans across my forehead, and he groans. "Fuck me or kill me...because I can't *not* be inside you one second longer."

His desperate admission races over my skin like

wildfire, making our touches frenzied, and in the wake of urgent caresses and hungry kisses, he's inside me. My body recognizes his. As he fills me, we fit together seamlessly. An ache blooms behind my eyes, the sensation in my chest crushing.

I ride him like that, slow and rhythmic, reacquainting our bodies and emotions. Listening to the desperate inhalations between us, an arrangement of harmonic sounds that strike my nerves like a tuning fork, the vibration an irresistible agony.

Every strum sparks an electric wave that threatens to crash over me as his hands roam from my breasts to my hips, mapping every plane of my body along the way, as if he's furious he can't touch all of me at once.

I know what he's suffering, the need to have him penetrating deeper, harder. More violent. Pain is the only answer when what you crave is so elusive, you can't physically grasp it.

My eyes drift open, and I catch sight of my hands circled around his neck. A fiery ember flickers beneath my skin, the lure to tighten my hold too seductive.

Alex watches me with a lurid mix of fear and awe. He bears down on the flare of my hips as he thrusts inside me, urging me to close my hands until I feel the rioting kick of his pulse against my fingers.

Some dark web of lust and wicked need grips me in a fit of madness, and I ride him hard, my movements salacious and wild, shamelessly abandoning any sense of morals and reservations. I can only see his pale-blue eyes, feel him hitting deep inside me—everything else falls away.

The raw emotion spiraling through me tears at reason until I feel the first peak of my climax. I cling to Alex, my hands strangling him to take life and fuse us together; just how I died on the cliff beneath him; I can't stop until we reach that pinnacle together.

He slams into me, bucking from beneath to either bring me to orgasm or loosen my chokehold. But every fraught attempt drives the consuming throb in my core deeper.

"Oh, god… Alex… Please."

I don't know what I'm begging for, what I need— but as he ruts against me, taking me higher, I feel the rumble of his forced grunt against my palms and, when I look into his eyes, his features strained with demand for oxygen, I shatter.

My back arches as he sinks inside me. My inner walls contract to hold him within, and my whole body ignites in a final burst as the orgasm crests and drags me under. My hands fall away. I hear his gasp for air, and it sends an arousing current of pinpricks over my flesh.

"That's it, goddess…take all of me." Alex doesn't relent. His forearm bands my lower back as he rises up, simultaneously crushing my hips to his. One hand braced behind him, he gains leverage to thrust inside me, rough and reckless, catching the fading wisp of my orgasm and fanning it.

My heart pounds at a dangerous rhythm. A sliver of fear slips beneath my rib cage, my chest wall threatening to crack. As my gaze locks with his, he understands; he senses my emotions firing out of control.

He runs a hand over my sweat-dampened hair, his mouth just touching my chin. "Don't run away," he says, "stay here. Let me take it for you."

I can only nod, but it's affirmation enough as Alex lifts me into his arms. He maneuverers me onto my back, then reaches off to the side. I close my eyes for a brief moment and breathe through the onslaught as I feel his body cover mine, then he shoves my hands above my head.

My eyes snap open as I feel the cool press of leather wrap my wrists.

Fear is a living force inside me. "Alex—"

He pulls the belt tight, binding my wrists together. Muscles aching, I struggle to bring my arms down between us, but he locks his hand around the knotted leather, trapping me against the stall.

Words fail as I stare into his eyes, a panicked quake rolling through my body to his. Alex pushes between my thighs, his hard cock settling right at the apex.

"I can't do this—"

"Trust me," he says, swallowing the remainder of

my plea as his mouth seals over mine, stealing the last dregs of my breath.

As he enters me, he grips the belt tighter, the sharp edges biting into my skin, reminiscent of the cuffs he used to restrain me during his electroshock treatment. It was the first time in my life I ever felt a complete and helpless loss of control.

As he releases me from the kiss, he thrusts deeper, his guttural moan affecting me on a visceral level. Every plunge inside me decimates, every coarse pass of his body against mine delivers maddening friction.

"God, you're so fucking perfect," he says against my ear. He locks his arm under my knee and positions me where he wants, in complete control, as he rails inside me. Relentless.

Alex fucks me until I'm coming undone, fighting against the belt, against the pleasure seizing my body— and the comfort I feel from being bound by him wrecks my sanity. But he keeps me tethered to him, not letting go.

"God-fucking-dammit…" He groans long and hard, his cock growing stiffer and ramming against my inner walls. "I want you to come. Right fucking now. Come on my cock, come with me—"

Back arched, I press against his chest as the orgasm takes hold, pouring through my veins like liquid fire as he rocks into me, thrusting hard once more to hold himself there until I feel the pulsating throb of his shaft as he comes.

He issues a torrent of curses as a hard tremor racks his body. He groans through his orgasm, pinning my body to his as he seals us closer, his mouth falling to my neck.

Feeling the intensity of Alex's surrender as he releases wrecks me on a primeval level, cathartic and empowering all at once. A thrilling warmth infuses my bloodstream—and I try not to put a name to what I'm feeling…but the damage is already done.

No other emotion can compare.

I close my eyes against the realization, allowing only a few tears to slip down my scarred temples before I'm able to regain control of my senses.

After an intense stretch of silence, where I feel the last delicious shockwaves recede from my body, I bring my bound wrists down along his back. His chest heaves against mine, breaths heavy and spent, as our heartbeats sync to a slower rhythm.

If this is love, it's the kind of love that makes you mad.

AFTERSHOCK

BLAKELY

*T*he beat of the music drifting through the walls has slowed, the volume lower. The club is winding down. Reality is a sharp whip as it lashes at the remaining fragments of euphoria. As the figurative smoke clears, the destruction is evident, and my body acknowledges every bruise and scrape.

Physical aches and pain and, what I assume is the nauseating symptom of regret, urges me to move. I shove Alex aside and roll away from him. He reaches for me, but I push myself up into a sitting position, using my foot to force the leather belt over my hands.

Once free, I stretch for my tank top lying next to his

head on the broken bathroom stall. The shirt is tattered and filthy. I ball it up and toss it aside.

"Next time, maybe we can actually do it in a bed," he remarks.

"That won't happen." Resigned on my clothing options, I reach for Alex's gray shirt and pull it over my head. His scent engulfs me, triggering a fresh ache between my breastbone.

I stand and clear the wreckage debris to locate my jeans, not wasting time to search for my panties. The creeper probably pocketed them, anyway.

He sits forward and grabs his shoulder with a groan. "Where are you going?"

I swipe my bag off the floor. "Somewhere...sane." The fact my mother's face springs to mind is alarming and proof I'm losing any rational grasp on reality.

"We still need to talk."

Aggravation rushes out on a huff of breath. "*Every*thing between us is done."

As he climbs to his feet, I lower my gaze to the floor, dismissing the uncomfortable surge of heat at seeing Alex's naked body, the clock on his leg a reminder of the danger we can't escape with the distraction of sex.

He steps into my path to barricade me from the door. "You can't deny what just happened between us, what I know you felt—"

"The only thing that happened was the need to get

my rocks off." I glance around the bathroom floor. Finding his pants and white undershirt, I scoop both up and fling them at him.

He catches his clothes, the pant leg smacking his face, which gives me more gratification than it should.

As he slides his leg into the pants, careful of the enflamed skin around the watch, he says, "It's not safe without me."

I arch an eyebrow, any argument I could make unnecessary as I stare at his leg to make my point.

He's the danger.

Everything Alex touches, he destroys.

"You need me," he says.

"I need you to get out of my way." I push against his bare chest, frustration thrumming hot and impatient along my nerves.

His hands circle my wrists, his fingers aligning with the bruised imprints he put there. "Blakely, there's no other choice. An actual deranged, psychotic serial killer is upset with the fact that we connected him to an investigation."

"Your investigation. *Your* bodies," I clarify. But what he's saying resonates, leaving ice in my veins to replace the lingering heat.

"Our bodies, baby. You're a killer."

The realization is quick and smarting, like tape being ripped away from skin. I'm tied to his murders because he *made sure* to connect me by copying the MO of Ericson's death. Which makes it look not so much like an unfortunate, random mugging.

"Oh, my god, you sick fuck. I couldn't figure out why you were targeting my revenge marks. Why you weren't disposing of the bodies. You did it to link us together. Some twisted union your demented brain thinks will…what? Unite us?"

He doesn't deny my allegation. "Your targets were meticulously vetted," he says in defense. "I could've wasted days or even weeks searching for new subjects."

"So it was a matter of convenience," I say, sarcasm layered thick in my tone.

A flash of annoyance passes over his features, and I twist my forearms free of his grip. He knows something more—he's keeping some vital piece from me.

"I have a plan," Alex says, but my thoughts are too far away to really hear him.

I'm searching the memory of my conversation with London for anything that was said, anything that was hinted to or—

I yank my tote around and open it. I plunder through the bag until I unearth my billfold and unzip the side compartment where I placed London's business card.

A confused expression crosses his face as I flip the card over and hold it up to the florescent light. "That fucking bitch," I say.

The card stock is too thick to see through, but I note the weight, then I tear it in half.

A small computer chip, like the tracker we used on the prostitute to mic her, is hidden between the thick card stock.

London bugged me.

I'm not sure if she can hear what we're saying, or if it's simply a GPS device, but I'm certain she's been spying on me. I told her about Alex killing his subjects with the experiment. Then Grayson shows up to torture Alex.

Wordlessly, I stalk to the broken stall and grab a wad of tissue, then proceed to wrap the chip. "Until I can learn more." I crumple the paper to muffle any potential feed and bury it in my bag.

"I'll analyze it properly later," Alex says, arrogantly making the assumption we'll be together.

I hold his gaze for a long beat. The weight of the shifting tide crashes down on me, and I'm trapped in his undertow.

Who is my enemy?

Should I run? Escape Alex? Escape the murders, the killers, and all the dangers suddenly hunting me?

Before Alex entered my world, I never ran from anyone or anything. But I already tried to run once, and I couldn't escape him. This time, I have to face my fears.

I don't know why London felt the need to spy on me. Maybe she gets off on interfering with her patients'—or prospective patients'—lives. Or maybe she's simply a pawn in a deranged trap orchestrated by her patient. Maybe we're all being manipulated.

Whatever the truth is, it doesn't change what we have to do—what *I* have to do.

I feel the warmth of Alex's touch as he takes my hand in his. "You're coming home with me."

11

LOVESICK

ALEX

$\mathcal{W}$hen a serial killer threatens to eviscerate you and feed your entrails to his pet fish, you start to evaluate your life choices.

By examining at a microscopic level, I can trace every decision and path taken, and the intersecting events, that create the perfect formula.

It's when I back out enough to examine the picture as a whole that chaos theory comes into play—the irregularities within my system that couldn't be foreseen. As always, the system's destination is decided very delicately by its starting point.

Had Blakely never contacted Dr. Noble, then it's likely Grayson wouldn't know I exist.

Had I never entered that night club, I never would've found Blakely.

Had I been less selective and chosen a subject sooner out of my typical selection pool, I never would've been tempted to enter the club in the first place.

I can keep tracing the path backward, noting each incident that brought us to this point, but there's a lesson in chaos: Chaos theory proposes a paradox, as it connects two familiar notions that are viewed as incompatible.

By any rational observation, Blakely and I are an incompatible notion.

And yet, she tore through my systematic world to obliterate me wholly.

She is the paradox.

Like the swing of a pendulum, her velocity and force is what I measure every need and aspiration by, and if I can only have her rage and hatred, then that is how I'll accept her. Having a piece of her is more consuming than any shallow connection.

Because I know we haven't yet reached our ending destination.

Like all systems, time is the variable that facilitates change.

And that anticipated change is a tense warning in the air around us. Having her in my space feels threatening, like at any moment she can shred the fabric of my feebly constructed world to decimate me.

Tonight proved she holds the power to do just that.

With her unstable emotions, she's a liability to more than just me; she's a liability to herself.

Instead of my selfish endeavor to repair my ego, I should've been engineering a compound to help regulate her neurotransmitters until her brain chemistry equalizes.

Since I have no ability to reverse time, I can only start from where we are now.

"You're sleeping in my bed," I tell her, as I clear the clutter off my desk.

Since Grayson is apprised to the location of both our places, it seemed only logical to utilize my previous unit. I have no doubt Grayson is aware of this residence also, but it's marginally safer, equipped with an alarm system and less entry points.

Blakely limps toward the closet and removes a fleece blanket, then tosses it on the beige sofa. "I'll sleep here."

A fiery thread curls beneath my skin. I rub the back of my neck to ease sore muscles and my growing irritation. We're practically war battered from fighting and fucking—maybe more so from the fucking—and still she refuses to admit the truth of us.

Her animated neural pathways have not affected her stubbornness.

Her hair is one wild tangle. She's still wearing my shirt. I have her scent embedded in my skin. The primal urge to bend her over my sofa and make her come until she admits her feelings rocks through me with crazed need.

I abandon the desk and storm toward her, every bruise and injury on my body rebelling against the movement. I reach her before she's able to mount a defense and scoop her into my arms.

"Let me go—"

"We've already established that's not happening." I carry her into my bedroom and drop her on the bed.

She grunts from the impact as she rises up on her elbows to send me a lethal glare. "I'm not your captive anymore."

"Would be safer for you if you were." I haven't completely ruled out locking Blakely up until the matter is handled. She wouldn't despise me more than she already does.

Although the loathing in her drained eyes states otherwise.

"Sleep on the floor," she says.

When she gives in to her weariness and lies back on the pillow, I remove her boots and toss them beside the bed. Then I yank the covers down from beneath her and gently draw them up over her body.

As I tuck the blanket around her shoulders, she

watches me closely, a curious draw to her shadowed features.

I've touched every inch of her body. I've worshiped her, memorized her. I've reveled in the feel of her as she came undone in my arms, and yet this delicate moment here is the closest I've ever been to her.

I can sense her guard lowering. She doesn't know how to shelter that fragile vulnerability yet, especially when she's exhausted and emotionally spent.

"There's nothing to fear." I chance smoothing the hair away from her forehead, and she lets me. "We're a force together. Your skills and my—"

"Psychosis?"

I choke off a laugh. "I prefer nefarious genius." I kneel next to the bed, becoming level with her. "They won't get near us. They can't."

After a weighted beat where I suppress the urgent desire to kiss her, I stand and start to move away. She reaches for my hand. Her fingers are light on my palm, but it's enough to stop me. I follow the connection up to meet her eyes.

"What did Grayson say to you?"

Stalled, I watch the reflected lights from the street play across the wall. Her vulnerability could be a manipulation tactic, a ploy to lower my defenses. Even so, I have to give in to her. We'll never reach our aligned destination if one of us doesn't yield to the other.

I walk to the window on the other side of the bed and close the blinds to shut out the city lights. Then I reach behind my head and tug off my shirt. I drop the ruined fabric to the hardwood before I slip into bed beside her.

I give her what she asks and openly recount my interaction with Grayson, even admitting to where he approached me. She knows I've been inside her loft; she's figured it out by now.

The groove between her eyebrows caves as deep as her thoughts. "I was right. They want us dead."

I lie facing her, my head propped painfully on my burned and bruised fist. "Logically, yes. Use us to remove any correlation to the victims, then remove all traces of me, the only link to my sister." Mary is the threat tying Grayson to the chain of events. Although the MO is different, authorities would have no issue drawing a parallel to The Angel of Maine for my crimes.

"And there can't be any witnesses," she says, piecing together her own demise as part of the equation.

"Letting either of us live would sabotage the carefully orchestrated vanishing act Grayson performed," I say. "He won't allow that to happen." Also, I believe he fears what such an exposure will uncover about his psychologist's involvement.

"But there's another variable I'm ashamed to admit I didn't consider, one the fiend himself was pleased to point out." I hedge closer to her, the sheet an annoying obstruction between us. "Brewster."

She gently shakes her head against the pillow. "I don't understand."

"The same software we used to spy on Brewster during the Ericson revenge job, Brewster can use to trace and find you. He may not be that tech savvy himself, but he has enough money and connections to find someone who is." I rest my hand on her arm, gliding my thumb under the shirt cuff to ground a connection. "Brewster is a danger to you."

Her skin pebbles with gooseflesh, and I try to rub the chill away.

"Why would—?" As soon as she starts to voice the thought, she realizes the implication.

"Money," I answer simply.

She wipes a hand down her face. "I should've realized. I would've realized it…before."

I draw my hand away. I could reassure her that her emotions will balance out, that she won't always be so aware of or distracted by them. But I let the silence build, fuming the bedroom like steam in the shower.

"I could hack Ericson's accounts," she says, thinking aloud. "Then I could transfer Brewster's money to an anonymous source, provide logins for him. If all he wants is his money, I can make that happen."

"He's being looked at too closely in connection to

Ericson's murder," I tell her. "Any transactions will be traced. It's too risky."

"I plan to turn myself in anyway," she says, staring at the ceiling. "It would just hasten the process."

Her confession doesn't distress me as much as the prospect once did. I watched Blakely pass a police precinct every day on her way to the martial arts studio. She'd pause in front of the building and stare at the door, and I knew what she was contemplating.

At first, I'd hover around a corner, waiting to intervene if she took a step toward that door. But as the weeks wore on, I rationalized this was only her process to alleviate the guilt. As long as she tells herself this is her course, then she can postpone as long as necessary.

We all lie to ourselves. Most lies are done for self-preservation. Our egos too fragile to view our insignificance within the universe candidly. Some lies are dangerous, when they delve into delusion to negatively impact others.

No matter what she needs to make herself believe, I will never let Blakely serve time for someone so vile and irrelevant as Ericson Daverns.

Taking into account her stubbornness, I don't reveal this yet. Instead, I want her reasoning to further the analysis. "What has stopped you?" I ask.

She rolls onto her side. Her look is molten on my skin. "I can't go to prison like this, Alex. I'll either go crazy, be medicated out of my mind...or I'll remove myself permanently. That's the only control I'll have."

The sounds of the city outside the window become a muted buzz of static as the air thickens with a tense charge. Blakely's threat is delivered with conviction, establishing a fear I wasn't aware existed.

"You have all the power," I tell her, handing over my control that easily. "You've always had it."

She maintains eye contact. "Tell me what you're planning."

I don't hesitate. "Frame Brewster for Ericson's murder. Then he'll go down for the rest of the kills." Which is why I linked the methodology to Ericson's murder in the first place. I didn't have a target scapegoat in mind at the time, but I knew I needed one for Blakely in the event she tried to confess to the murder.

In that regard, Brewster is the perfect fall man.

She flops onto her back. "Right. Giving Grayson what he wants, while eliminating Brewster as a threat."

"If there was ever a contender for the dark triad on the dirty dozen scale, it's Brewster," I say. "He's an elite psychopath. He has no connection to my sister, therefore the authorities won't draw a connection to Grayson. And with Brewster behind bars, he's less likely to establish any connection to you for Ericson's murder."

"Less likely," she repeats, then drops her head my way. "You like your numbers. 'Less likely' isn't math you can accept. You're holding something back."

My gaze drifts over her captivating features, and I want nothing more than to lie to her, to let her believe we can eliminate our problems so easily. Ultimately, if she'd agree to leave with me right now, fly to another country and vanish, the whole situation would disappear and resolve itself.

However, selfishly running away won't help her realize her potential.

Red seeps through the bandage on my hand, and I lift it before blood can stain the sheet. "I should redress my hand," I say, but her soft touch on my arm—that skin-to-skin contact—prevents me from moving, from even breathing.

"Just tell me," she says.

"You're right," I say, inspecting the damage to my hand. Blakely took advantage of my weakness, which reaffirms what I'm about to tell her. "Brewster won't take being framed so gracefully. He'll dig until he finds what he needs to mount a defense, which means you'll always be in danger—" I lift my gaze to hers "—as long as he's alive."

She sits forward and links her arms around her covered knees. "You're forgetting that I'm confessing to the crime, which completely voids that hypothetically absurd idea anyway. So, what else do you got?"

I fell in love with her fire, so much so I welcomed the burn, but in moments like this, her obstinance makes me want to either punch a wall or pin her to the bed.

"Memory and time," I say, sitting up to join her. "They're a bitch. You can't undo either, and you can't exert control where you're at an equal risk of losing it."

The same infuriating impatience must plague her as she shoves her fingers into her hair. "Alex, what the hell? Don't speak to me in riddles tonight."

"You can't confess to Ericson's murder," I say. "They won't believe you."

Her gaze travels to me, and it's there in her stunned expression, the understanding between us. She knows I'm capable of altering evidence. If she hasn't already figured out why I targeted the victims on her list, then she's piecing it together now.

"I can still try," she says, attempting to call my bluff. "A confession from me, the person hired to take revenge on Ericson, would be enough to muddy the water." She shrugs. "And if nothing else, it would alleviate my conscience."

I run my hand over my hair, anxious to treat my hand. "You can always try, and you might even succeed. Or you could wind up in an institution. Someone with a weighty title and influence, like the renowned Dr. Noble, could make that happen easily enough."

She throws the covers off and slips out of bed.

Battered and bone-weary, exhaustion plucks at my patience. "Come back to bed."

"I'm leaving," she says, searching for her shoes.

"Maybe I'll just get out of this whole fucking crazy city."

I toss off the covers and climb out of bed. I have her in my arms before she's able to get to the bedroom door. Her fight is weak; she gives up easily as I band my arms around her. She's just as exhausted as I am.

"Look at me." The serious tone of my voice makes her instantly look up. "You're a justice dealer."

Her brows pinch together as confusion mars her features. "What—?"

"You took Ericson's life in that alley because he needed to die," I tell her. "Revenge, justice, balancing the scales… However you want to define it, it's in your makeup, your DNA. From the first moment you fought back against a bully on a playground, you knew your course, Blakely." I expel a heavy breath, softening my tone as I raise my hand to push the hair away from her face. "There was a moment, somewhere before we met, that you questioned *when* not *if* you'd ever take a life. You knew at some point, revenge wouldn't be enough."

She's still—too still—some mix of fear and shock and maybe even relief washing over her. I release her, removing my arms to give her space, but stay close.

She doesn't deny what I've said. I know this about her, because I've studied her psychopathy and her personality type, and yes, there's a chance Blakely never would've committed murder.

But there's a greater chance she would have.

And in that event, she wouldn't have had the emotions and self-preservation to protect herself.

After a tension-filled beat where we gauge each other, the silence declaring all the confessions either of us refuse to reveal, she swallows, blinking as she resurfaces from the turmoil of her thoughts.

"I always thought I could stop myself," she confesses.

I inhale deeply, her scent abrasive as I sear it into my lungs. "You might have."

"I'll never really know, though, will I," she says. "Not now."

But she does know. And I deserve all her outrage and condemnation, but I'm not the only bad guy in her life.

I'll let her use me as her punching bag, though. Whatever she needs. She can put all the blame on me, and I'll take it for her. Just like I'll take the pain she needs to inflict so she can make love.

"No matter what you chose to do in a nanosecond in that alley," I say, "the fact of the matter is Ericson was the real monster. He never would've been prosecuted, maybe never even seen the inside of a court room. He never would've stopped hurting women until someone stopped him. Permanently."

She rubs the fresh bruises wrapping her wrist, her gaze cast downward. As she brings her eyes up to meet mine, my chest is hit with the impact of her softness, the cruel vulnerability she now suffers, leaving her open and exposed.

"You were saving a life," I say to her, trying to reach her. "You've been so focused on the life you took, you never think about the life you saved that night."

Her gaze shimmers with the wetness of unshed tears, and I ache for her, wanting to bring her into me, but scared to lose this moment.

She blinks, then wipes away the trail of tears streaking her cheeks. "I hate this feeling," she admits. "I want to turn it off."

I cup her face and stroke my thumb across the fresh stream of tears. "You saved her life," I say again, because she needs to hear it. "So I won't let you lose yours."

Inhaling a shuddering breath, she pulls away and tucks her hair behind her ears. Just like that, Blakely has learned how to transition her emotions. "And then what? After we complete this insane plan of yours, Grayson just simply disappears from our life?"

The way she says *our life* gives me a deranged level of hope I'll keep fighting for.

I stay honest. "Grayson is more of an obstacle, more of a threat to us than Brewster. He needs to be removed."

A spark of understanding lights her eyes as she stands before me. "If you get rid of Grayson, then you have to get rid of London."

I nod once. "I've considered that."

"She might be an innocent," she says, crossing her arms to shield herself. "Sometimes, women can't help who they fall for."

I read too much into that statement. She notices, and glances away.

"Grayson, London, Brewster…" I trail off, my gaze dropping to her mouth, her body a seductive lure as she allows me to draw her seamless against me. "All obstacles have to be removed."

After a tense heartbeat where we stand locked together, she finally connects with my gaze. "I'll help you get rid of Grayson. I'll help you remove all the obstacles. Then you're going to fix me, Alex. Whatever the risk."

I touch her cheek, skimming the backs of my fingers across her delicate skin. "That's a cost too high."

She grabs my hand. "That's the price you pay for playing God."

"We'll see."

"That's the deal, Alex. Either you agree, or I walk away from all of this, from you—"

"I'll agree to your terms," I say, "but I need collateral. Something to ensure you won't make a rash decision."

She shakes her head. "Like what?"

"Like the switchblade," I say, gauging her wary response. "I want the murder weapon."

Realization opens her expression. Pushing her hands between us, she slides her palms up my bare chest to break us apart. "It's the only evidence that will prove who killed Ericson."

"It's what we need to frame Brewster." *It's what I need to ensure she's never tied to the murder.*

A moment of indecision, where she glances at the bedroom door, then she releases a resigned breath. "Fine." She rubs her arm as she crosses to the living area, saying over her shoulder, "I didn't feel safe leaving it in my apartment." She digs through her bag.

A sprig of anger shoots up my spine, coiling my bones in tension. She's had the evidence to put her away on her person this whole time. "That's exceedingly dangerous, and selfish."

Stalled in the bedroom doorframe, she cocks her head. "Oh, was I supposed to leave it in my apartment for you to steal? You're right, how selfish of me."

I walk toward her and hold out my hand. With stoic acceptance, she lays the plastic-wrapped knife in my palm.

"I'll put it somewhere safe," I say.

"Or, you can cut that fucking thing off your leg," she counters.

I almost smile, hearing some of the tough Blakely slipping through her weakened cracks.

"Help me," I ask her.

We look at each other, the insinuation clear I'm asking for more than her help with removing the watch.

"But obviously, not with this." I set the switchblade aside on the dresser and head into the bathroom, returning with a roll of bandage and a razor blade.

"No wire cutters?" she says, sarcasm hedging her tone. "Damn. This is going to be painful."

And it is painful. But not unbearable. As I lie on my back and observe, there is something so darkly erotic about watching Blakely wield a blade. The way she traps the corner of her lip between her teeth as she concentrates. How focused she is on the task, almost absorbed, never flinching with sympathy, never squeamish.

I might worry she's experiencing some form of residual setback from the procedure, reverting to her former self—but it's like watching a surgeon operate rather than a butcher dismember. Blakely is finding a way to channel her emotions to override the erratic extremes.

If she can utilize this strength for what comes next... I have to admit, it's exciting me just thinking about it.

Once the offending object and its incessant ticking has been removed, Blakely stares at the clock face, some faraway look clouding her eyes, before she sets the razor blade on the nightstand.

She flips the antique Rolex over, inspecting the backing. "You should take it apart and see if there are any surprises waiting for when the clock strikes the looming hour."

But I'm no longer interested in clocks or threats. I reach out and take the object from her hand, toss it on the bed. She's braless under my shirt, and I swear she never looks sexier than when she's wearing my clothes.

While she was removing the wires, I felt nothing— no pain, no tension, just the misery of being so near her, watching her nipples rub against the thin material as she worked, a tantalizing tease that I can't touch her whenever I want.

Which is all the time.

I lift my hand to her face and use my thumb to clear away a smudge of dirt on her cheek. We're still filthy from dirty sex in a dirty bathroom. "Take a shower with me," I say.

Her eyes hold mine, my request loaded with far more heated desire than simply getting clean.

"Yes," she breathes.

I want to taste that word on her lips.

Blood rushes to my groin. I lunge forward and tear the shirt over her head, then I have her in my arms and off the bed, carrying her to the bathroom.

As I reach for the wall switch, she catches my hand. "Leave the light off."

I hesitate momentarily before moving toward the glass shower. Keeping her in my arms, I flip on the spray and wait for the water to warm.

She tentatively touches the fresh dressing over my hand. "How did this happen?"

I turn my gaze on her, absorbing how soft she looks in this moment. "I was saving what was important to me."

She arches a brow in question.

"Your journal," I say, holding her gaze.

I managed to save both journals. The one I kept on Subject 6, with all my recorded findings and sketches of Blakely, and the pages she wrote while being held captive—the ones I kept tucked in my journal.

But, even though her data was important, it was her pages I risked reaching into the fire to save, her thoughts I couldn't bear to lose.

Somehow, as she studies my features, her eyes searing through my façade, I think she knows this.

She aims her attention on my hand and begins to remove the bandage. "You shouldn't get this wet."

After she drops the bandage, I set her feet to the floor. I meticulously peel the rest of her clothing away before I remove the other bandage wrapping my calf.

Her gaze tracks the bruises and scrapes along my chest. I can feel the raw claw marks that rake my back from her nails. My face bears the marks from her fist. We're both covered in contusions and injuries—our bodies a canvas exhibiting passion and violence.

You can't love the tormented and not accept their pain.

I drag her into the shower and kiss her under the rain of water, like I kissed her under the waterfall. I kiss her like I'm deprived of air, like I'm drowning, and she's the only pocket of oxygen amid the water.

And she kisses me back with enough vengeance to rock a torrential storm.

The warm water stings the fresh cuts, my calf on fire as water cleanses the open wound, sending a swirl of pale-red blood around the shower base.

I grasp her waist and plant her back to the tile. As she locks her arms around my neck, her breasts press enticingly against my chest. I graze my fingers down the flare of her hips and shove my throbbing cock to her pelvis, groaning over her mouth at the feel of her heat and the abrasive rub. She's all bare pussy, but the hint of growth against my dick feels so damn good, driving me crazy with need.

Bending at the knees, I lower myself and slip my cock between her thighs, grinding my shaft along her smooth, wet lips.

Her breathy moan slips free to torture me, her hips undulating seductively to lure me right over the fucking edge of sanity.

I hook an arm beneath her knee and drag her thighs apart, notching myself at her entrance. She writhes her hips, the sexy motion begging me to sink inside her.

I grip the back of her neck and angle her face up

toward mine. "Just tell me one thing," I say, a plea whispered over her mouth.

She blinks up at me, beads of water seductively slipping down her face. At her bated silence, I expend a restless breath. "Are we making love?"

A forceful swallow drags along her throat. "Alex—"

"Tell me you love me."

Her gaze flits over my features before she casts it down at the shower floor.

"Christ, Blakely. Tell me you want us—"

"I don't want to do this alone," she admits.

A searing ember of regret constricts my throat. I did this to her; I made her alone, suffering an ailment no one on the planet has ever suffered. Until she adapts, I'll take her abuse readily. Some sick part of me even craves it.

Which is the only reason I can justify what I say next. "You think I wanted to want you? That I wanted to fall in love with you? I loathed myself for my weakness. Some desperate part of me even wanted the treatment to kill you, so you'd no longer be a temptation."

I expect her to look as stricken as I feel from the glutted confession. Yet, when she lifts her gaze to mine, her features are soft, a river of pity tucked behind a portrait of empathy. "At least you're finally being honest," she says. "That's the sanest thing I've ever heard you say."

I expel a harsh curse, my lungs on fire. Grasping her

face, I angle her mouth toward mine, the frantic need to make her feel my torture a monster rattling the cage. "When this is done," I say, baring the absolute honesty she craves, "I want you to cut my fucking heart out with that razor blade."

At least then she'll have her revenge, and I can die peacefully, captivated by her.

Because for me, it's only her. There can never be anyone else.

Only her.

The slight quiver of her lips reveals her hesitation, but before I can fully comprehend what she's feeling, she crushes her mouth to mine. The kiss is an assault. Raw and aching from hours of abuse, she punishes my lips.

I hoist her up against the tile wall as she wraps her legs around my hips, fusing our bodies into one before either of us can stop.

I'm inside her, filling her to the fucking hilt, trying to fuck away the pain and regret threatening to tear me apart.

I know what has to be done—and god, she'll despise me even more, but I saw the doubt welling in her green eyes. I know what's running through her head.

I'll don my villain hat to keep her safe.

The darkness presses against us, sheltering us from the past and the future, a moment in time carved out just for us. We become a tangle of limbs and desperate touches, vying for an intimacy past the barrier of our flesh.

Frustrated, I growl against her mouth as I rail into her, not able to get close enough. "I want more," I say. The double meaning of my words pulls at the last frayed thread to unravel my patience.

But for once, I want her in my bed. I haul her drenched body to the bedroom. Her legs stay locked around my hips as I drop us to the mattress, our skin slick and heated, her body inviting me in as I capture her mouth in a brutal kiss.

I compete against gravity as I thrust into her. I fall so completely into her that the world bleeds away, leaving us encased in the fiery throes of our pain and darkness.

12

THE HATTER

BLAKELY

*T*he morning sun is a laser beam that wants to fry what's left of my brain cells. Two hours of sleep isn't enough to function on, especially when every other hour was spent abusing my body, in more ways than I care to recount in the light of day.

Some part of me felt guilty as I walked out of Alex's apartment. I've never believed in lying to myself; didn't know it was possible, actually. I always pitied people who did. The disturbing truth is, I felt comfort in his arms, in his bed. I felt safe sheltered in his embrace beneath the spray of the shower, protected. It's irrational and twisted, like a victim imprinting on her abuser.

It's true that daylight clarifies what the night

TRISHA WOLFE

obscures.

Hidden by darkness, every desire and lascivious, forbidden act is heightened, and it's easier to shut our eyes and let our resistance cave, to reach for what will sate the burning hunger.

An ache sears beneath my rib cage, but I push on. The blare of horns and the screech of brakes greets the early morning as I cross the bustling intersection. I'm unsure if the pain is physical or psychological, or an anguished combination of both.

I expected the guilt of giving in to my weakness for Alex to be the deciding factor—but strangely, as I watched him sleep, sun-illuminated dust particles dancing around his still form, all I felt was hollow.

That void lingered inside me like an annoyingly obsessive quirk. Like when you second-guess if you shut the gas off on the range, or when a song lyric gets stuck on a loop in your head but you can't remember the title.

This ill feeling in the pit of my stomach might be regret...but as I have little experience with regret, it's a tune I can ignore.

Because when the sun shown in Alex's room to wake me, I was already decided.

Damn the consequences, and damn the fallout for Alex.

It's time to end this.

Last night, when he began plotting the deaths of

186

three people, and the excited flutter of adrenaline sparked my bloodstream, I knew his claim about me was true; there was already a darkness inside me before he damaged my brain.

I've known this since my second-grade teacher tried to teach me about cruelty, when she glimpsed the festering sickness of my nature.

I heard it whispered to me on a street corner when some random, nameless stranger tried to snatch my purse. I felt it curl around my insides and tickle a craving, tempting me to act on the deranged threats I slung at him.

That guy saw it in my eyes. That's why he ran away.

Alex saw it in my DNA. That's why he chose me.

And when Alex confessed as much last night, whatever frail but hopeful thread I'd clung to of returning to my former self unraveled, plunging me below the deepest level of vulnerability.

Even if Alex could accomplish the impossible and return me to who I was, I was broken before.

Only an insight afforded by my new emotional awareness could reveal this raw truth.

So I clung to him in the darkness of the shower instead, trying to fill a void that's always been inside me. And for the faintest moment, I think I did, or maybe this is the first lie I've told myself.

Whatever the reason, the fact remains: I'm dangerous.

Whether it's due to Alex's procedure or not is irrelevant. I've hurt people. I killed a man. If I didn't force myself to leave Alex sleeping in his bed, when he rolled over and looked at me, when he kissed me again…

I would kill with him.

I would be lost with him.

Taking a fortifying breath, I stand before the entrance to the police station. I've passed this building every day on my way to the martial arts studio. I've stood outside and watched people enter and leave, waiting for the moment I was brave enough to take a step forward.

Last night, I knew I had to confess, and I knew it had to be today. Before Alex has the chance to frame Brewster, or makes the grave mistake of double-crossing Grayson.

I also knew walking out of his apartment with the murder weapon wasn't going to be easy.

My only choice was to make Alex believe I was committed to his scheme, to him. I needed him to trust me, utterly, implicitly. And…I can't continue lying to myself. It wasn't all an act.

I've battled my confusing array of emotions for Alex too long, and I was so weak, wanting one night to lose myself to these overwhelming feelings and passion, to experience a connection with him and know it's real —before I end us.

But that's even more reason to be standing here now.

The greater danger lies not with me, but in the two of us together.

The morning air is hazy and dense, sticking to me like a thick film, the secret I've been carrying around a callused layer I need to shed. Once I walk through these doors, I'm not coming back out. I'll be detained. Read my rights. Put in a holding cell. I've never been arrested before. I've always found ways to skirt authorities.

This will be a whole new experience.

Targeting Alex in this manner is drastic and self-sabotaging. But truthfully, it's killing two birds with one large river stone. I'll be reprimanded for my crime, and Alex will be stopped.

He said I'm a justice dealer, and justice will be served.

Confessing to Ericson's murder is not even about the guilt—I had rules, limits. Even as a psychopath, I had a moral fucking compass.

I inhale a steadying breath laced with car exhaust and sidewalk garbage as I take a step forward, and my phone vibrates in my back pocket. Halted, I give in to the nagging compulsion to check my phone.

A text message from my mother: *I've retained a lawyer for you. Call me.*

My hackles raise, and a nauseous sensation hollows

out my stomach. I move to the side of the building and call her.

She answers in a lighthearted tone as if she doesn't see my name on her screen. "Vanessa Vaughn."

I release an impatient breath. "What are you talking about?"

I can hear her audible exhale over the line. "Blakely, please. Lower your voice. It's been taken care of. That's all you need to know." She pitches her voice an octave higher, like she's simply making an appointment at a day spa. "I expect you for brunch today."

An invitation for brunch from Vanessa is not a casual summons. "I don't understand what's happening, but I have to go."

"I know where you are right now," she says, her voice taking on a stern edge. "I've sent Patrick to fetch you. He should be arriving shortly. We'll discuss this once you're here."

I glance up to see my mother's driver pulling to the curb across the street.

"Shit." I end the call and walk toward the crosswalk, but my gaze is drawn to a suited figure in the backseat of the car, and I immediately stop.

My whole body ices over. Time suspends as our eyes meet. That piercing gaze I stared into while feeling him inside me, that I've craved with both fear and longing. A clash of emotions war within me, my heart beating at a frenzy.

I step off the curb toward the car, never taking my eyes off Alex. Last night could've been another one of my dreams; I'm not even sure if it was real.

I'm drawn to him by the tethered cord between us. Terrified to look away, frightened to reach him, a swirling vortex of emotions drowning out the honks and shouts as vehicles brake and swerve.

Arms wrap my waist and I'm hauled out of the street.

"Let me go—" I elbow Patrick's ribs, but he tightens his hold despite my struggle. My body remembers every bit of abuse I put it through as pain webs my muscles.

I've lost sight of Alex. Searching madly, I feel like a wild animal who just lost their prey.

"Miss Vaughn, it's not safe," Patrick says as he sets me on the sidewalk. Mouth thinning into a hard line, he grabs his side. "Are you okay?"

His question is weighted with more than one meaning of my current state.

"I'm fine," I say, distracted as I lock gazes with Alex in the car. I shake my head, then look at my mother's driver. "I'm sorry. For your ribs."

He blinks, stricken by my apology. "It's all right, Miss Vaughn."

When I look over to find Alex, I'm torn between storming toward him and running in the opposite direction.

I don't know how the hell he managed to orchestrate

this—but I should never be surprised where Alex is concerned. And yet, every single time, he finds a new way to shock me.

Patrick opens the passenger-side door of the Audi. "Let's get you home."

His voice draws me out of my thoughts and I close my eyes briefly, making a decision. I pass the passenger door and open the backseat door, sliding in next to Alex.

He brushes his finger over the back of my hand. "I always have a contingency plan," he says in a hushed tone.

I stare straight ahead. "You brought my mother into this," I say, snatching the seatbelt and buckling in. "You don't have a plan. You have a death wish."

I glimpse his boyish smirk from my peripheral.

First, I'll handle Vanessa. Then I'll take care of the mad scientist.

I can only deal with so much crazy at one time.

"To the witch, Patrick," I say.

Patrick's grin is evident in the rear-view mirror as he puts the car in Drive. "Yes, ma'am."

It's an ambush.

As I enter the rooftop terrace of my parents' three-story Park Avenue penthouse that overlooks an expansive view of the city, I see Rochelle lounged near the plunge pool. She's having a mimosa with my mother. Both of them recline on white chaises, like it's not a weekday morning.

"I have no idea what's going on, but this just looks toxic." I immediately start to leave, and it's Rochelle who hops up to stop me.

"Sit your scrawny ass down and shut it," she snaps, literally snapping her fingers and glaring through a giant pair of expensive sunglasses.

"How did you get pulled into this?" I quiz her.

"Oh, I'm sorry. Was it some other Blakely Vaughn who called me at three a.m. looking for a ride to Manhattan?" She takes a dramatic sip of her mimosa, and the crystal flute *tinks* her glasses.

I deflate a little. I did call her for help after I escaped Alex, and she was there for me. "You're under a covered pergola, Rochelle." I glare at her obnoxious sunglasses.

"UV rays, honey. You'd do good to think about that." She takes her seat again and lounges dramatically, downing a healthy sip of her drink. "You're not going to be young forever."

"Unless you feed me some of your immortal blood." I smile brightly.

Rochelle looks at my mother. "She's so your daughter, Vee."

Vanessa only sighs, as if raising me (something my

nanny did more so than her) was such a burden. "You should be taking this seriously, Blakely."

I press my lips together, gaze pinning her with severity. "And what *is* this, Mother?"

She sets her champagne flute down on the marble accent table and removes her glasses. Her eyes are a mirror reflection of my own, a sight that stills my blood. "I told you your little hobby…job…whatever you want to call it—" she waves her hand dismissively "—would someday get you in trouble. Now a man is dead, and like a nitwit, you think you can just walk into a police station and hand yourself over." She exhales an exasperated breath and palms her cheeks, as if the strain from her speech stretched her chemically-peeled skin. "Honestly, Blakely. What are you thinking?"

The pavers beneath my boots fall away, the shift in gravity throwing me off balance. My gaze swings to Rochelle with an accusatory stare.

She shakes her head. "Don't look at me. I'm far too self-involved to keep tabs on you, sweetie."

I nod and lick my lips, the lingering taste of my night spent with Alex hitting me with bitter resentment.

Shoot me up with Ketamine and abduct me. *Fine.* Lock me in a basement in the middle of the wilderness and do mind-altering experiments on me. *Fine.* Make love to me and make me feel like I'm losing my sanity. *Fine.*

But sic Vanessa on me like a spineless snake to do

your dirty work…

Not fine.

I glance through the glass railing and into the penthouse, trying to track his movements. Having Alex in my family's home is disconcerting. I don't spot him, and I wonder if he's perched on a balcony with a creepy pair of binoculars and listening device. Or maybe he's spying on me with a drone.

Which are suspicions that should be ridiculous, unless you've become the object of obsession for Dr. Alex Chambers. He knew exactly where I was this morning. He knew exactly what I was about to do. Which means…

I pull my phone out from my back pocket and drop it to the pavers, then smash the heel of my boot into the screen.

My mother glances at the destroyed device before she looks at me with a disapproving frown. "I see your temper hasn't improved."

I stare down at the shattered phone. He "made love" to me in his bed. He made me believe it was possible for me to love him. I *hurt* this morning when I struggled with the choice to turn myself over.

And at some point during the night, he installed spyware on my phone. Everything he professed last night was bullshit. There can never be any trust between us. His only concern was preventing me from entering the police station, so he involved my mother.

An act of evil in and of itself.

I cross my arms and glance between the two conspiring women on the terrace. I could deny everything. I could claim Ericson's death was an accident or self-defense. But for some reason, the relief I feel at having someone else know my secret strips a layer of guilt away, even if those persons are my mother and the most narcissistic client on my roster.

"How did you find out?" I ask Vanessa.

My mother purses her lips. "I got a call from your lawyer," she explains. "Josh Vanson. He called me and explained your circumstance, and said it was time for an intervention before you made a very bad decision. Thank God I got to you in time."

Anger sears my nerves. Alex plundered through my bag. He found Vanson's business card. Not only did he lie to my mother about who he is to manipulate her, but he's also made her an accomplice. She's aiding and abetting a murderer.

I can't let him hurt my family.

"I'm surprised he didn't tell you he was my lover," I say, shaking my head. "He's not a lawyer. He's a delusional stalker. You need to get him out of your house."

My mother's heavily mascara'd eyelashes brighten wide. "Lover? Are you dating? How serious?"

Of course, that's what she hears. I give Rochelle a pleading look. "Help me."

Rochelle is busy tapping her phone screen. "Are you sure? He looks like a lawyer to me." She flips the screen around to show me the website of one Josh Vanson, JD. A picture of Alex in a business suit and looking very lawyer-y is positioned at the top of the site.

Christ. I rub my forehead, feeling as if I've been sucked into an alternate universe. Alex coded a redirect link for the real Vanson's website. But of course he did.

My mother waves her hand. "But what he told me about what happened with this revenge job of yours—"

"You believed him," I supply for her, to make the confession easier.

She pulls her linen wrap around her shoulders. "I won't lie, Blakely." A dead silence follows, underscoring the blank.

I nod slowly. "Right. I'm leaving now."

Rochelle bounds up and snags my arm, pulling me to a stop under the pergola. "You once told me *no killing* was rule number one." She releases my arm to remove her glasses, her weathered eyes finding mine. "I don't know what happened between you and that dead man, but I know the girl you are. Whatever took place, that piece of shit probably had it coming. And neither me nor your mother are going to allow you to throw your life away over some…man."

She spits the word like it tastes bad in her mouth. I suppose it does, considering her seething hatred for her ex-husband.

I glance at my mother, at the woman who I have never been able to form a connection with. Not all her fault, as I was born without the capability. I'm sure at one point, she may have even tried.

She stands to join us. I see a rare tremble in her lips not caused by an injection. "We'll make it go away," she says, as she touches my arm. "I may not be able to fathom all the details, but I know my daughter. Whatever has happened, we'll make it go away."

An even rarer feeling presses against my chest, the weight causing my eyes to burn and an ache to clog my throat. The sudden onset of this new emotion induces a moment of panic, and I have to look away to conceal the moisture in my eyes.

"How can you make it go away?" I say to her, blinking a few times before I can meet her gaze again. "You can't buy innocence."

Her painted eyebrows wing up. "Blakely, you're still very naïve when it comes to money. You can buy innocence, and you can even buy guilt."

I shake my head, confused. "I don't understand…" I let my thoughts trail off as the steely resolve in my mother's eyes issue a threat.

"I'm sure whoever is truly at fault for this heinous crime will be found soon." She links her arm through Rochelle's for support. "Then this whole mess will be behind us."

And like that, Vanessa Vaughn is at the pinnacle of

the food chain once again.

Rochelle raises her champagne glass in mock toast. "To the unlucky bastard. May he roast in hell."

My head spins as a startling revelation becomes clear. Alex's plan to frame Brewster. By bringing my mother in on it, he's forcing my hand. He's made her a culprit, which means I have no choice but to go along with his scheme.

In order to protect her, I have to get her away from here. From me, from Alex. From serial killers and dangerous criminals. "Mom, this is insane talk. Why don't you go on a cruise with Rochelle instead?"

She scoffs. "Listen here, Blakely. Who do you think handled your father's business and his connections? You think luncheons and cocktails built half of New York?" She steps close to me and lowers her voice. "My daughter will not be destroyed because of some crooked, raping financial adviser."

My breathing shallows, a buzz hums in my ears, muting the sounds of the city. The severe coolness in her green gaze sends a chill over my skin. How does she know so much about Ericson?

"Listen to your mother, honey," Rochelle says, breaking into my disturbed thoughts. "This city talks. Money knows money. Let us protect you."

"Yeah, okay," I say, but I'm only half listening as I catalog the events of this morning. Alex didn't have time to reveal the whole situation to my mother. Ericson

Daverns had a reputation—one my mother was apprised of, but not through her network of trophy wives.

"You knew who my clients were," I say to her, the implication heavy in my tone. "You…had access to them. You kept tabs on them."

She lifts her chin, clears the fringe of bangs from her forehead. "It's a mother's job to make sure her child is protected. Whether she appreciates it or not."

I glance at Rochelle, then back to my mother, stunned. "The past six weeks, you've known? And you didn't say a word to me?"

A flash of guilt settles in the makeup creases of my mother's features before she expertly smiles the expression away. "Would you have told me the truth?" she demands. "Had your lawyer not contacted me—"

"He's not my lawyer," I snap.

"You have never once accepted my offer of help," she continues, undeterred. "Had…whoever-that-man-is not contacted me today, you would've made a grave mistake, Blakely. The whole situation was already handled."

"*How*?"

She shrugs, as if getting your daughter out of a murder charge is simply another socialite duty. "I didn't need to know the details. Like I said, I know my daughter. I also know there was a victim, a woman, who needed a little financial padding to persuade her memory loss."

She was unconscious. The woman Ericson attacked in the alley, she was knocked out. I swear, I checked. I made sure she was alive, but she didn't see my face. And even if she did get a glimpse, she was traumatized. Memories can't be trusted. There's no way she could pick me out of a lineup.

"Mentally combing through all those loose ends?" My mother sips her drink smugly. "You're welcome, my daughter."

My mother paid off the victim. Which means she had a way to locate her. Someone on the inside of the investigation. An officer, or a detective. Or even the fucking police commissioner himself.

I'm at a loss for words, which I can't say has ever happened before when it comes to Vanessa. "Thank you," is all I manage to say.

"Of course." Her expression softens as she studies my face. I'm sure my display of emotions is more than unsettling for her. She sighs, then: "You weren't in any serious trouble. That woman only recalled your description as a witness to her attack. Someone reached out to me, and I just made sure your name wasn't mentioned anywhere near the investigation."

Because she knew Ericson was my revenge job. Because she knows her daughter is a psychopath. Because, even though she wasn't sure, she thought I might have killed a man.

Then today, Alex confirmed her assumption.

"Now," she says, "let's call for brunch. I need to soak up some of these mimosas before my pedicure appointment."

But before she heads inside, she adds, "Oh, one more thing." She rakes her nails through my highlighted tresses to untangle the strands over my shoulder. "Vanson, or whoever that man is inside my penthouse, he knows more than he should. So…try to make good use of him. He does have good bone structure. Who are his parents?"

I shake my head lightly, not at all surprised that, for Vanessa, my love life is more dire than murder. But, she has surprised me at least once today.

I've never asked for my mother's advice before, so it's foreign and tastes strange. "How would you handle him?"

Rochelle releases a throaty laugh. "If you don't know how to handle him, then you're damn clueless. Because it's written all over that boy's face how he wants you to *handle* him."

My mother sighs. "Blakely, you've been limping around my terrace, wearing a necklace of bruises that could only come from sex."

"Rough, filthy sex," Rochelle retorts.

"He obviously called me this morning out of concern for you," my mother says. "That means all the power is in your court—"

"*Balls*," Rochelle interrupts. "It's balls in her court,

Vee. At least two of them." She winks at me before sliding her sunglasses in place.

Vanessa makes an impatient sound. "Try to enjoy the part of life that's not all about work and revenge," she says. "Have your fun. Just don't let him anywhere near the press when you're done with him."

In other words, Vanessa Vaughn has very little concern for the man in her house. In truth, this very moment, I find my mother more terrifying than Alex or even the Angel of Maine. And I'm pretty sure her last statement was a veiled threat to keep Alex quiet.

She kisses my cheek, then Vanessa's mask slips back into place as she turns to head inside. But for a moment, she let me see the nurturing yet fearless woman beneath, and that's the reason I turn toward Rochelle and say, "She trusts you."

"As should you, honey. Women in this city stick together. Too many old boys clubs and bell jars. We're not letting one arrogant penis ruin your life."

Crudely, that might be the most endearing thing she's ever said to me.

"There's more than one arrogant penis," I say, casting my gaze toward Alex standing near the glass slider of the garden room. I return my gaze to Rochelle. "You're going to get my mother out of the city for the next two weeks."

"So you can get yourself into more trouble?" She quirks a pencil-drawn eyebrow.

"So I can know she's safe."

With tight lips, Rochelle nods. "Sure, sweetie. I knew you had a heart buried beneath those perky tits somewhere."

"Yeah, who knew," I deadpan.

She kisses me on my other cheek before she departs behind Vanessa. "Oh, a little advice for whatever you're up to—" she swivels around "—enemies are plenty when it comes to money. Keep your enemies close, and if they get out of line, call in your mother." She cackles as she heads into the penthouse.

I brace my hands on my hips and stare down at the crushed burner phone. If my mother and Rochelle knew the whole truth, their advice would be much different… and Alex might find himself buried under Vanessa's rosebush.

However, there's been enough confessions and reveals for one day.

The scar tissue on my palm pulses, suddenly making itself known. I rub my thumb over the jagged skin, recounting my talk with London and what she revealed about the bodies—Mary's victims.

A peculiar calm settles over me, similar to the moment when I'd figure out the perfect scheme for a client's revenge, like when the puzzle pieces suddenly all come together.

SHEAR PASSION

ALEX

I watch Blakely enter the garden room through the glass slider.

All beautiful, restrained fury, she says, "You went too fucking far."

Maybe.

But she should realize by now there are no lengths I won't go to in order to protect her, to keep her mine.

I finish shaving off the thorns on the stem, then hold out the red rose to her. "I like your mother," I say, decidedly skipping over the part where we argue a moot point. "I don't know why you don't spend more time with her. She's fascinating." I glance around the opulent garden room. "I can see you in a place like this, raised with wealth and the finer things in life. It suits you."

"Yeah. Cold, unfeeling, shallow." She snatches the rose from my hand and tosses it to the Carrara marble floor. "The personality I used to have."

"I'd reason you still do," I say, setting aside the shears, "seeing as you stone-cold left me this morning without even a Dear John letter."

"This isn't a game, Alex. You involved my mother."

I wipe my hand over my mouth. I hadn't planned to involve her to this extent, but turns out Vanessa Vaughn knows more about her daughter than Blakely realizes. Once the call was made on the spoofed number, Vanessa couldn't be placated by simply having Blakely diverted for one day.

She legitimately seemed to care about her daughter's welfare, a detail Blakely led me to believe was the opposite. Truthfully, I wasn't prepared for the authority Mrs. Vaughn commanded over the situation. But, seeing as Blakely's plan has been effectively thwarted, and her mother has entrusted her into my care, it seems to be working out for the best.

"I told you, turning yourself in wasn't an option." At her incensed silence, I assure her, "She'll be safe. The sooner we resolve the issue, the sooner your mother's worries will be assuaged, and her involvement won't have to go any further."

Her features draw together as she steps toward me. "Are you threatening her?"

The insult smarts. "I know trust is difficult, but after last night, you shouldn't question my motivation. I would never intentionally hurt you, Blakely."

"Trust?" She narrows those sea-green eyes on me. "You put spyware on my phone. How's that for trust?"

A desperate measure I had to take. I sensed her uncertainty last night. With her volatile emotions, I couldn't risk losing her again. And I couldn't risk she'd do exactly what she attempted to do this morning, not with a deranged serial killer threatening us.

"I will do whatever it takes to protect you," I say. "Even from yourself."

She closes her eyes and shakes her head, aptly displaying her frustration. "What are you wearing?"

Her segue throws me, and I look over my dark-gray Versace suit. "Dress for the job you want, or the job you want others to believe you have. Something to that vein. I'm your lawyer now."

"You're so delusional, you don't even know who you are anymore."

I step around the bench, reaching her before she can recoil. I cup her face between my palms, ensnaring her eyes with mine. "I'm the man who burned his life down for you. I'm the man who will take a life without question if it means keeping you safe, and I will have no measure of guilt or regret, because I'll stop at nothing to keep us together."

Her gaze flits over my face searchingly, a flicker of panic present in the depths of her eyes. "And you're still just as insane."

My mouth tips into a crooked smile. "Love is madness, baby."

I was crazy for her the moment she stole my breath at the bar, and every action since has been a battle within myself to accept that she owns me.

Why else do we take and steal and covet, if not to possess the person who torments us?

I took. I stole. I coveted her.

In trying to set her free, I only discovered what a greedy monster I truly am. After experiencing her give herself over to me last night, to keep her in my world, I'll pillage and destroy like my neanderthal ancestors.

I will be the villain she needs.

I feel the force of her swallow against my palm, and my thumb runs the length of her neck, admiring the bruises I put there. She felt that passion between us, and even now, in the light of day in her mother's garden room, she can't deny it.

"I want you to let me go," she says.

I breathe a light curse. "Or I could take you right here on this bench." I move in closer and feather a kiss along her delicate skin, inhaling her arousing scent that goes straight to my cock.

"You're so fucking crass now," she says, though I can feel the tremble of her body.

I smile against her neck. "Starve a man, and he becomes a wild beast." I drop a kiss to the hollow of her throat before I straighten and meet her gaze. "Tell me you want me."

She releases a soundless laugh. "Never happening."

"Tell me you love me," I demand.

"In your sick fucking dreams."

I collar her throat, feeling her pulse kick against the web of my hand. "Then the more you starve me, the more depraved I'll become."

Her eyes flare, and I can sense she's about to spit in my face, so I open my mouth to catch the insult, then capture her lips, sinking my teeth into the kiss. She groans and pushes against my chest to break free.

She wipes the back of her hand across her mouth, smearing a red stain. I touch my lip, realizing it's my blood. She bit me back. Harder.

"Let's get this over with," she says.

I suppress a smile. It wasn't my intention to manipulate her, but leveraging her erratic emotions does get her to focus.

"It's easier to let yourself feel only one emotion," I say, as I pull out my phone. "When you start to sense any loss of control, anger subdues the fear, doesn't it?"

She smirks knowingly. "Actually, it works great. All

I have to do is think about smashing your face, and I'm in complete control."

I hold her livid gaze, my body heated as I'm tempted to make good on my threat to bend her over the bench. I reach down and shamelessly adjust my hard cock.

Blakely's eyes never leave mine, but the quick rise and fall of her chest reveals her arousal, and I smile before lowering my gaze to my phone screen.

With a deep, calming inhale, I check the latest update on Brewster. He's scheduled to fly to Canada in five days, not leaving us a lot of time. I flip the phone around to show Blakely the itinerary.

"We'll start with Brewster," I say. "He has a deadline."

"Fine." She wets her lips, trying to destroy what fragile restraint I possess in this moment. "Right after I buy another burner phone and get Vanessa out of the city."

She's still worried about her mother, even though she's masking that fear by directing her anger toward me. Some part of me may be a tad delusional when it comes to her, but she was so close last night...so close to accepting us.

The greatest love stories are born of fire.

Tragedy. Cruelty. Passion.

I wasn't searching for love; my analytical mind never believed in the concept, nor did I think it applied to my life. A romantic partner would be a burden, would prevent me from achieving my goals.

But Blakely has always been different. She's unique to me, my other half. Now that I've found her, I can't simply return to a gray existence with no purpose.

She's my future. Whether we're making love or trying to kill each other, obsession presents as love and grips you whole.

I have no choice but to keep her.

Whoever claimed love should be healthy is a fool who believes in greeting cards.

All love is selfish and feeds ego. Our mind's way of keeping us relevant in a world that doesn't care if we jump off a cliff.

As such, I did what I had to do today to prevent the woman I love—that I *need*—from jumping off her cliff.

I slip my phone into my pocket and cock my head. "This morning, you needed incentive," I say. "Do you think Grayson or Brewster or any of his thugs will stop with just you? They'll come after your family to get what they want."

She levels me with a fierce glare. "Which you made sure of by implicating my mother." She grabs the shears off the workbench and approaches me. "Chicken or egg, Alex. Which came first?" She takes hold of my tie, drawing me closer. "Would anyone be in danger if I'd never met you?"

She snaps the shears, cutting my tie off below the knot.

Tossing the garden tool on the bench, she turns her back to me and heads toward the door. "Grayson gave you two weeks. I'm giving you five days. Then I want you out of my life forever. Or else next time, it won't be your stupid tie."

At her threat, I shift uncomfortably at the twinge of pain in my cock.

Devising the plan was relatively simple. I just had to decide which psychopath I wanted to frame for the murders: Grayson or Brewster.

Elimination is the objective.

In order for Blakely to remain clear of any implication to Ericson's murder, all three players—Grayson, London, Brewster—need to be removed from the board.

And in order for Blakely to accept her new path and existence, she needs to embrace her design.

She's the perfect calibrated weapon, after all.

Her years spent honing her skills in the art of revenge, coupled with her extreme emotions, fashioned a masterpiece not even I could've imagined.

Victor Frankenstein would either be impressed, or terrified by my creation.

But with her unstableness at this early stage, I have to go slowly with her. In essence, direct her toward her main objective without overloading her system, as was the case with Ericson.

I was too weak at the conception of my project to accept the truth. The end result was never going to be about curing psychopaths. Grayson said it himself, a cure is not realistic. No, it's not about curing him at all —it's about killing him, and all others like him.

After all, that is the only true method to cure the world of psychopaths.

My failures with every other subject helped me realize why Blakely was a success, and how I need to utilize her rarity.

The moment she gave in to her overpowering emotions and took a life, she flipped a switch in her DNA. Her genetic makeup is that of a killer. All the proof was there in her brain scans. When compared to those of infamous killers, Blakely's scans were very closely matched.

She was right that we'll never know if she would've crossed the line prior to the treatment. Most psychopaths never commit murder. Brain scans can't predict future actions.

But as I stare at her from across my lab, watching the way she examines my workspace, taking in every detail, I know undoubtedly I was meant to find her.

The fates wove our life threads together, and now

we're bound to one another—creator and creation—whether by fate or doom. That is our future.

I remove my glasses and set them next to my laptop. Ever since we left her parents' penthouse yesterday, she's been distracted, detached. Plotting the scheme used to be her favorite part of her revenge jobs. I know this plan is extreme by comparison, but I need to figure out what's holding her back and remedy it.

She notices my attention on her. "You were this close to me the whole time, just a few blocks away." She turns and hoists herself up onto the gurney. "I could sense you watching me. What's that called again? You told me the first time we met."

"Scopaesthesia," I say, though I never told her the actual name of the phenomenon, just remarked on how she was highly attuned to the ability to sense being watched. Another of the skills in her arsenal which makes her perfect.

"Right." She nods slowly. "Alex and his big, smart words."

Pushing back in the metal chair, I cross my arms. "We should go over the plan."

She hops off the gurney and wheels the stool Grayson last used to the metal table, evidently ready to participate.

I put my glasses back in place and look at the screen. I have dates and locations recorded based on what I gleaned from Brewster's schedule. Which, of course, can and probably will change over the subsequent days. You can't count on a career criminal to keep to his Google calendar, but it should give us enough information to map his next steps.

Deciding on the order of events came down to behavior. Brewster is an ideal victim for the Angel of Maine serial killer. He runs a drug ring, pumping toxins into the city. So a simple trap designed around a supplier who's forced to overdose on his own supply—while not as gruesome as some of Grayson's kills—is believable. And that's all it needs to be.

Planting the switchblade on Brewster is one step further to tie him to Ericson's murder, putting the final nail in the coffin. Grayson punishes a seedy, murdering criminal, and the detectives have a closed case on both sides.

"Grayson will expect a move like this from you," Blakely says, folding her arms on the table.

I close the laptop. "But not from you." I reach into my rucksack and remove the microchip she discovered in Dr. Noble's business card. "It's not a listening device. It's a tracker. Any reason you can think of why Dr. Noble would want to keep tabs on your whereabouts?"

She begins to shake her head and stops abruptly, her dark eyebrows knitting in thought. "London seemed to think you would find me," she says. "Maybe it was a way to keep tabs on you."

Possibly. But Grayson had no issues tracking me

down, and here I am, right in the same place where he left me. My own deduction is that Grayson has every intention of disposing of me when the countdown is over. He's aware of my feelings for Blakely, and he can assume I'll try to hide her before that happens.

He also took my USB drive and the remaining vials of my compound that, to a psycho killer who mocks a cure, holds no interest for him. But maybe it interests Dr. Noble. Killing Blakely might not be their endgame.

I keep this theory to myself for now, and lay the chip on the table. "Did you pack a bag?"

"I got everything I needed from my place," she confirms.

I made sure Blakely cleared out her apartment of anything important yesterday while I analyzed the chip and did the groundwork for Brewster. Five days to frame two people for murder leaves no margin for error. We can't lose any opportunity that may present because one of us isn't prepared. Even to run.

Besides, Blakely staying with me has added benefits.

"But you didn't comment on my answer," she says. "Which means you have your own secret theories as to why London bugged me."

I steeple my fingers together and hold her inquisitive gaze. "I think there was something said in your meeting with Dr. Noble that sparked her interest." I can't give her more than that.

She rises from the stool and walks to the factory window to peer out. After a lengthy beat, she says, "London did mention something strange during our conversation." She turns to look at me. "About Mary."

My sister garners my complete attention. I stand and push my hands into my pockets, suppressing the urge to check the time. "And what was that?"

"Just that, during a session, Grayson told her where Mary disposed of the bodies of her victims. Not the exact location. But I knew where."

Alarm shoots through my bloodstream, ice-cold. "Was that all that was discussed." My voice is gravel. A demand, not a question.

"I found the bones, Alex," she says. "When I escaped the fire, I fell right into them." She holds up her hand, revealing a red scar along the side of her palm. "Are the remains your subjects? Your sister's victims? Or both? Because I think Grayson is very thorough when it comes to learning all the pertinent details of the victims he stalks, don't you? Like where they bury the people they murder."

As she lowers her hand, I look away.

Fuck.

Without thought, I drive my bandaged hand through my hair, and a throb of pain comes alive. I walk toward the other side of the room. I need a moment to think, to process. There are always complications. This doesn't have to change the plan.

"Are you going to answer me?" Blakely makes her own demand.

I turn to her, deciding the answer she needs can't be sourced from her series of questions. "What do you want to know?"

She blinks, then tucks her hair behind her ears, suddenly looking so endearing, I can't deny her anything. "Whose bones are buried near the river, Alex?"

Inhaling a fortifying breath, I lift my chin. "Mary put her patients there," I answer her honestly. "And I added to the graves."

Her lips thin as she presses them together in thought. "If we get rid of Grayson first—"

"No." I wave a hand dismissively. "If he knows the location, he already has a failsafe in place to expose the bodies." I know this, because it's exactly what I would do. Leverage. Even if I'm giving him too much credit and no one is alerted once Grayson disappears for good, it's a risk I can't chance.

I failed my sister once.

I can't have her name splashed across the media again as the remains of victims are unearthed.

The faint *snick* of a ticking clock drifts to my ears. "Shut up."

"I didn't say anything," Blakely says, and I catch her wary gaze.

I rub the back of my neck, my nerves stretched tight.

"It's my problem," I tell her. "I'll figure it out." Which sparks my curiosity. "Why are you helping me?"

Arching an eyebrow, she says, "Has your paranoia disintegrated your brain?" She marches over to the laptop and flips the top open, displaying the countdown I have set at the top of the screen. "If the deranged duet has put this much thought and preparation into you, what do they have planned for me? As much as it pains me, we're stuck in this together. Solving your problem solves mine and now my mother's. Because believe me, if getting rid of you would fix my life, you'd already be tossed into the Hudson."

I blink at her, my mind delving as I follow her train of thought. "All right, that's it."

She shakes her head. "What's it, you crazy fuck?"

"We need to remove the evidence," I say. Not as simply or as carelessly as dumping the remains in a river, of course, but getting rid of the evidence just the same.

The only way to ensure Grayson can't reveal the victims is to remove the bones. Yes, there will be trace evidence, but not enough for authorities to warrant reopening an old case to try to track down the remains.

"I won't be a part of this," she says, her tone just shy of self-righteous. "Those are people. They have families. They deserve to be given back to their loved ones—"

"If you truly believe that," I interrupt her soapbox

speech, "then why didn't you report the remains yourself?"

Her silence infuses the room. I nod, accepting what she's unable or unwilling to voice. She will never admit her reasoning but, she presumed the bodies were my subjects. Her feelings for me prevented her from lashing out against me in that capacity.

I reasoned early on why she never went to the police after she escaped the cabin, why she didn't make a report of her abduction. Blakely doesn't like attention. She would find an investigation invasive. It would expose her own unethical revenge jobs—but also, she's battling the confusing feelings she has for us.

All those intrusive questions cops ask would force her to think about our time together. What we said. What we did. The intimacy we shared.

It was easier for her to move on in denial, ignoring the bones' cry from the grave, rather than face her own conflicting emotions. She had so much to deal with already.

Instead of pointing this out to her, I walk toward the window, to the same place where she stood a moment ago, and look out over the city. "Relocating the remains isn't ideal. I need a proper disposal method. I need fire."

"You could always have another meltdown and burn the rest of your cabin to cinder," Blakely says, her tone impatient.

"That wouldn't generate the kind of heat..." I trail

off as what she says registers past my confliction. I swing around her way and remove my glasses. "The rest of the cabin?"

She pushes her hands into her back pockets. "Sorry I don't know the proper heat level. I've never had to burn a body before." But her chiding doesn't distract from what she said.

Placing my glasses on the gurney, I move toward her with measured steps. "You went to Devil's Peak."

She crosses her arms, and my gaze leisurely travels over the marks on her wrists—the marks we left on each other as we imprinted our fury and yearning. "I had to know if you were alive," she says, a revealing tremor in her voice.

I stop walking. I'm a meter away from her, but suddenly there's no distance at all.

She's the one who takes the final step to reach me, and my breathing stalls in my chest.

"What did you feel when you didn't find me in the ruin?"

Head canted toward the floor, she says, "Relieved."

It's a wisp in the air—the frailest tendril of promise—but I reach for it as I clasp her chin, tilting her head back so our gazes connect.

She had the evidence I was alive, and all the evidence she needed right there buried in the valley's earth to turn me in and permanently remove me from her life, and yet she didn't. She hunted me. She found

me. She fought so hard not to submit to her desires…
and it's right here, now, between us.

One profession from her will decimate me.

"Ask me to kiss you," I say.

She licks her lips, ensnaring me. "Kiss…my ass."
But her voice holds no malice. She's shivering in
eighty-degree weather.

I release her chin and graze my fingers along her
jaw, spearing my fingers into her hair. "I'll eagerly kiss
your ass and every inch of your body," I say, "even
when you vehemently deny what you want, when you
fight it, I'll give you what you need." I lean down
closer, feeling her breath slip over my mouth. "And
you'll help me destroy the evidence."

Her eyes flare and, without words, she consents with
the slightest nod of her head against my hand.

This is what she requires; I understand now. With
the smallest nudge, our systems start to align. Chaos
begins to harmonize.

She's never needed anyone before, never had an
emotional need to be met, and she doesn't even know
what to ask for, or how to ask. And from me? The
villain who bestowed the cursed emotions on her? She
can't surrender.

But I'm the only one who can give her exactly what
she needs.

When her emotions run high, when she falls into

that dark chasm of emotional turmoil, I'll lace our fingers together and pull her away from the brink.

I'll let the friction between us spark and roar until we're nothing but spent embers.

Passion can only burn us alive once.

"A crematorium," she says, as if picking the thought from the air around us.

My brow furrows as my thoughts circle to where we began. "That would be convenient." I lower my hand, caressing down to the base of her lower back. "Unfortunately, I don't have access to something that convenient."

Her swallow drags along her throat. "I do."

She doesn't give me time to ask. She presses into me and crushes her mouth to mine.

And as we evolve from a fiery collision to forming molten matter, we forge the darkest of plans in my lab. Sirens wail and horns shout, the sounds of life outside these brick walls flood the dilapidated space while we plot how to silence the dead.

14

TIME'S UP

ALEX

*B*lakely's presence hums next to me, my skin abuzz from her nearness, her energy. Both the physical closeness and the metaphysical. She still has reservations—ones that will take time to climb over the inertia I created along our timeline, but there is one constant in the universe, and that's change.

Nothing stays the same forever.

Like the turn of a dial, one emotion gives way to the next along the spectrum, and as time passes, our emotions shift and modify. One kiss shouldn't be life-altering, but factoring in Blakely's stubborn disposition, that kiss was shattering—a magnitude eight earthquake to rock our foundation.

After the sun set, we headed into Chelsea, where the flurry of nightlife thrives, but the cover of darkness shrouds us as we move through the veins of the city. I follow Blakely as she turns down a familiar alleyway. I was just stalking this borough as we pursued the same target and yet, somehow, I missed the connection.

I don't believe in fate.

But I can't deny the irony.

Blakely stops outside of a three-story building with two-tone bricks and a faded black awning.

The awning reads: Pet Heaven Crematory.

She looks at me expectingly. "I watched Addisyn enter and leave here," she says, turning toward a lockbox nested alongside the rusted door. "She was never one for discretion." She starts to punch a code into the keypad, and I grab her wrist.

"Cameras," I warn.

With a derisive tilt to her head, she says, "You're not a very diligent stalker," before she returns to the keypad. "The batteries on the Wi-Fi cams are dead. I checked them the first day while trailing Addisyn."

The box beeps and she opens the small black door, producing a key.

I glance around the bustling four-lane street. No one is watching, no one cares. Who breaks into an animal crematorium? Still, I can't ignore the tension knotting my spine.

"This is too exposed," I say, even as she pushes the door open.

"You're too accustomed to your habitat. Your private, creepy forest. Well, this city is my forest. I know how to operate below radar." Leaving the lights off, she uses her phone as a flashlight.

The interior looks like what I'd assume the average pet crematory would look like. Miniature caskets. Bare brick walls with a few display shelves to showcase picture frames and animal toys. A generic desk. The smell of linseed oil used to polish the wood mingles with a dry fragrance of what I presume is ash. Another distinct odor hovers beneath of animal feces. I curl my lips.

The front of the business is set up as a merchant shop, with urns and picture frames, even wooden boxes with inscriptions. I suppose mourning pet owners want to bury their pets like a loved one, with memories and cherished objects, as they place them in comfortable, satin-lined caskets and watch them roll into the cremation unit.

Blakely stands over the desk, her light aimed on the laptop. She slips on a pair of disposable gloves and flips it open. "I'll check to see when the next cremation is scheduled."

Which leaves me to explore the unit itself. I take out my phone, making sure it's on airplane mode so I'm not pinged in this location. As I push through the double doors into the back, the pungent scent of antiseptic stings my nose. My reservations are high for this course of action.

There are ways to produce the degree of heat necessary to incinerate remains rather than taking the risk to transport bones into the city, and then unload them into a building. Where anyone can become a witness. There are too many unknown variables and contingencies; nothing feels within control.

I'm a scientist. Solving problems with science is what I do. Before I even inspect the unit, I'm decided against this method and am in the process of turning around when a sound pricks my ears.

The telltale *tick* of a second-hand reverberates through the dark room.

I stop moving, aware of the unnatural silence, the absolute blackness pushing against me from all corners. Focusing on the sound, I try to decipher if there's an actual ticking wall clock, or if it's a manifestation of my anxiety.

My calf suddenly aches. The louder the sound grows, the more intense the pain. Like the phantom pain of a missing limb, the ghost of the antique Rolex reminds me that our time is limited.

The neurotic need to find the source threads my muscles, and I light my phone as I coast farther into the room. I should be attentive to the sounds in the front— Blakely's movements, the front door, possible trespassers—but I'm attuned to the clean *snick* slicing the air, drawing me toward the center, where the light catches on the gleam of an object.

I stand frozen.

My lungs burn as I claw for a breath, the pressure damn near cracking my chest.

I'm in the dark room of my cabin again. The walls pitch as coal, the only light source stemming from the mounted pendulum clocks that appear to float all around. There's a familiar weight in my hand. Not comforting, but habitual, like getting a hit of a drug you can't bleed out of your system. Toxic, but alleviating the bitter pang of homesickness.

I know what the object is…but I also know it's impossible.

I destroyed my pocket watch.

I killed the tormenting demon in my head.

But it's right there before me—hovering mid-air, spinning in slow oscillations to the rhythm of the relentless ticking. I lower my phone as I approach my pocket watch, trepidation slowing my steps until I'm right up on it, the clock face staring into mine.

As I reach for it, a loud *clang* shatters the trance. I whirl around, my guard shooting up like a high-rise.

Blakely stands in front of me, her hands pressed to the grids of a chain-link door.

She snaps a padlock into place, the harsh *click* detonating around us as her eyes never leave mine.

Awareness begins to trickle in past my stupor. I watch Blakely turn her back to me, then after a moment, the overhead lights illuminate the space.

I glance around as all five senses absorb my surroundings at once, piecing a very twisted puzzle together.

When I look at the suspended watch again, it's still there. The timepiece wasn't a hallucination. With a twinge of apprehension, I grasp the pocket watch with a trembling hand, realizing the hands of the clock aren't moving. The time is set to the exact moment I struck the watch with a river rock.

Forever stuck.

Just as I'm stuck where Blakely trapped me.

In a cage.

15

THE VILLAIN

BLAKELY

"The watch doesn't work. It's still broken," I tell Alex, answering one of his obvious questions as he reverently touches his pocket watch where I strung it from the top of the crate.

I doubted this would work, luring Alex into a literal trap with a literal dangling carrot. The idea seemed comical to me yesterday. But I knew if there was any carrot tempting enough to transfix him for even a second, it was the pocket watch he destroyed. The one I unearthed at Devil's Peak.

"I didn't really have time to have it repaired," I say. "And really, I wasn't sure if I wanted to. I always hated the fucking sound of it. So I opted for this instead." I hold up my phone and point to a small Bluetooth speaker positioned on one of the wall shelves.

I tap a button on the phone screen, and the rhythmic ticking stops.

"Clever," he says, but he's only partially invested in my explanation as his fingertips graze the polished pewter. "You did replace the glass face, though."

Pocketing my new phone, I walk around the cage, giving it a wide berth. "Had to make it enticing."

Alex suddenly backs away from the watch as if it might explode, his eyes trailing me as I head toward the speaker and pack it in my bag. I can practically hear the gears turning in his big brain as he processes his predicament.

"This isn't a crematorium," he says, touching the cage mesh.

I stand on the outside looking in. My hands still gloved, I cross my arms. "No, Addisyn doesn't work at a crematory. Like you said, that would've been just a little too convenient." I nod to the many crates lining the walls of the room. "She works at a dog kennel. The perfect place for locking up a misbehaving pet." I slink closer to the cage. "You're out of control, Alex. You need a timeout."

His mouth tips into an endearing smile, so out of character for this moment, my hackles raise. "Then what?" he asks.

I pull out my phone and send a text before meeting

his penetrating blue eyes. "Then I'll decide what to do with you."

This is the first time I don't have a plan even slightly mapped out. With only half a day to strategize, half a day where Alex wasn't watching me every second, I had to improvise.

During our meeting, London gave me a critical piece of information when she revealed Grayson's knowledge of where Alex's sister buried her victims. I knew Alex would be more than alarmed over this revelation.

Of course, relocating the bones from Devil's Peak couldn't have been my idea. Alex would've been way too suspicious if I volunteered that solution. I had to set him up with just enough fear, prod him toward his own selfish justification, in order to get him to take the bait.

I admit, offering the crematory as a disposal means was sloppy on my part. I thought he would know right then I was up to something, so he needed a distraction: my feelings for him. One kiss—one moment of vulnerability—was enough to get him this far.

In the end, I had to trust London's assessment of Alex, that his obsession with me—his masterpiece—had dictated his course. He couldn't see past his desperation, his ambition. While he was stalking Addisyn to find me, he didn't notice the details of her life, not when he was obsessively involved in mine.

While I was "packing" my loft, I contacted Addisyn and made a deal.

I offered her life back in exchange for her assistance. I'd remove the Internet bots, I'd restore her name and delete the offending evidence, if she did what I asked. No questions.

She agreed immediately. She closed the kennel for renovations and sent the animals packing. I'm not sure how she accomplished this, and I don't care. I just need one week. At my instruction, she covered the awning sign with a cheaply printed Pet Heaven Crematory to change the name, and rearranged the shop entrance to appear like a crematorium rather than a kennel.

And she agreed to one other stipulation in order for me to reverse the damage of the revenge scheme.

The double doors swing open. Alex and I both look toward the doors as Addisyn enters the tense room. I glance at Alex to see the confused draw of his eyebrows as he tries to work through this twist.

"Let me enlighten you." I head toward the wall of green lockers. I open one and select a large syringe and two vials of Acepromazine —what the groomers use to sedate the dogs. "Addisyn is going to keep watch over you while I handle some things."

"Some things" is a vague reference to the serial killer and his psychotic psychologist, but I don't have to spell that out for Alex.

"You don't keep tranquilizer guns here?" I ask Addisyn to my left.

She pries her suspicious gaze away from the cage and looks at me, incredulous. "That's illegal."

I arch an eyebrow, indicative of what she's a party to right now. I hand her the syringe and drugs. "Don't be sparing. Dose him good," I say. "And don't let him manipulate you. If he gets that crate door open—"

"I know," she says. "Trust me—" she fires a lethal glare at Alex "—no one is preventing me from fixing the shit-show my life has become."

At least there's one certainty I can count on: a narcissist will selfishly do what's necessary for their best interest. No matter who they have to hurt.

Addisyn won't wrestle feelings of guilt where Alex is concerned.

Not like me.

Even after what he's done to me, made me suffer…I might hesitate if I have to put him down. And one second of uncertainty will be all it takes for him to gain the upper hand.

Alex captures my gaze. He pushes his long-sleeved shirt up his forearms as he moves to the cage door, then curls his fingers around the mesh grids. "Your feelings for me scare you this much," he accuses.

I roll the gloves off my hands. "Addisyn," I say, "I need a moment alone with the pet."

"Sure…" After she sets the bottles and syringe on the counter, she pushes through the doors, leaving us alone.

"She'll fuck up whatever you have planned." His coy smile falls as his tone lowers to a serious base note. "You involved her. She knows too much. You're making a mistake. But it's not too late. We can still fix this."

"By killing her?" I shake my head as I shove the gloves into my pocket. "I can handle Addisyn, and I can handle Brewster, for that matter. I devised revenge schemes long before you crashed my life. Just ask Addisyn herself." I swing my bag over my shoulder. "And I can do it without having to kill." I blow him a goodbye kiss. "Be a good boy while I'm gone."

"You're coming back for me."

I stand halted, weighing if I should treat his statement as a question or declaration, and ultimately decide to ignore it.

But then I almost forget. I pivot back toward the cage and drop the bag. "Empty your pockets."

Alex holds my gaze, his fingers threaded through the square mesh of the cage. "I just wanted you to realize your greater purpose."

"You wanted to make a psychopath terminator," I fire back, a hoarse laugh slipping free. "I may be sick, Alex, but you're deranged. One of us has to be sane and put a stop to this."

His fingers tighten around the metal; he despises not being in control. Of this situation, of me. Finally, he relents and shoves away from the cage. He digs into his pockets and removes the items one-by-one.

He pushes a pocketknife through a square opening, dropping it into the bag. His wallet comes next along with his phone. He slides both under the slat of the wire crate. He produces the microchip we discovered in London's business card. Hesitantly, he palms the chip a second before sending it through the cage.

I catch it before it hits the bag. "Your belt, too," I order him.

An amused sound slips free as he unbuckles his black belt. He then winds it slowly around his uninjured hand, making a production for my benefit. Heat prickles my face as I recall the feel of the leather tightening around my wrists.

"I'm pretty crafty with fabrics, too," he says. "Want my clothes? Leaving me caged naked and humiliated for a week might balance the scales between us."

I lift my chin. Of course Alex would conclude a week timeline, considering Brewster's departure schedule, but it's his assumption I'll simply release him at that point that sends a fire-hot lash across my skin.

After he slips the belt through the slat at the bottom of the cage, I kneel down and toss it in the bag and zip it closed.

As I stand, I meet his eyes, knowing every torturous emotion exposed on my face is impossible to mask.

"I'm not trying to punish you, or to get even," I admit, startled to realize it's the truth. "You were right, Alex. When you told me I was only focused on the life

I took rather than the life I saved. If for nothing else, thank you for helping me realize this, and to understand what I have to do now to save another life."

I let my fingers rest on top of his, swallowing the burning ache that rises up in my throat.

Maybe it's the sincerity he hears in my voice, or the lack of resentment, but his features relax, and a look of solemn acceptance settles over his expression.

As I pull my hand away, I catch sight of the suspended pocket watch. I'll let him keep his token. When he crushed the watch, he was trying to set me free. Or he was trying to free the both of us. Either way, he was attempting to rid himself of the madness devouring his mind from the experiment and the lives he took.

Breaking the timepiece didn't change his outcome, however.

I'm not sure if anything can change for us, but he should have the reminder.

As I start to leave, he finally speaks up. "Grayson took the USB drive with the compound formula."

Paused at the doors, wariness threads my spine. I close my eyes and breathe, steeling my resolve. I can't fall for his manipulations.

"They want you," he continues, undeterred. "To study you, or to experiment on you… I don't have a working theory yet. But they do want you, and I'm positive they will inflict far worse tortures than I ever could."

"That's a chance I'm willing to take." I leave, not looking back at him.

"Even if you pull it off, they're not going to just let you go. I'm trying to protect you—" he shouts after me. "This can only end bloody."

It's possible he's telling the truth, as far as he believes. The other night in the dance club, I wondered what London and Grayson were after, if it was me who lit the fuse and set off the chain of events. I could continue to speculate but, as I've learned from Alex, too much theory and becoming mired in analysis can inhibit action.

And I'm at my best when taking action.

I palm the microchip, my resolve firmly in place as I pass Addisyn on my way out. "Do what you have to." I stop at the front door, glancing her way. "Try not to kill him, though. I like his pretty blue eyes."

She cranes a perfectly shaped eyebrow in acknowledgment, and I wonder if I've made the right choice.

Doubt is a debilitating emotion. Doubt makes you weak, it makes you question your own mind. Even when you know the right choice, the friction to make that choice holds you back.

The pain and heartache that comes from strength of character is the price you pay for your morals.

Sometimes, it's easier to give in to your fear.

I hate Alex for what I've become, but right now, I hate myself more.

I leave Addisyn in charge of Alex, with the hope I can pull off a scheme to finally set us free. Because that's all any of us want.

It's what I read in London when she spoke of her patient; her desire to be free—free of the constraint of her world, free to be with Grayson. For them to live their life on their terms.

Alex is a threat to that.

He threatens to expose Grayson, and no matter how well organized Alex's plan is, we can't risk failing. We can't take any more lives.

If I succeed, I can deliver freedom for all of us without becoming the monster Alex tried to create.

16

CHECKMATE

BLAKELY

*M*y phone vibrates in my back pocket.

I dig it out to read the text: *He's starting to get ripe.*

Aggravation knots my shoulders at the countless interruptions. I stretch and fire off a reply text to Addisyn. *Hose him down.*

We're talking in code, I suppose. If anyone ever finds it necessary to comb through my data, I'm simply discussing a smelly dog with a woman who works at a kennel. I did manage to take this into account before I decided to lock a man in a cage and embark on a reckless mission to frame one of the most dangerous men in NYC.

It's taken four days to orchestrate a strategy which ties Brewster to Alex's victims and...mine. Ultimately deciding to frame Brewster for Ericson's murder was the part which took the longest. I had an internal battle to wage.

However, for the frame job to be clear-cut, there can't be any loose ends or victims sharing the same murder methodology as the other victims. Every death has to be linked to Brewster's drug ring.

How I did it:

I meticulously scoured Ericson's financial reports and bank statements, highlighting any transactions connected to Brewster's shell companies. The obscene number of 0s Ericson was moving for Brewster made me realize Alex was right in the regard that Brewster would come after the person who killed his financial advisor.

He would have to know the *why*, and if that person had knowledge of Brewster and Ericson's dealings, whether for blackmail or another nefarious reason. It was simply too risky for Brewster to ignore, but also, there was money piling up in accounts with no one to move it.

This is where the motive comes in.

With one smartly coded program, all those dirty 0s were transferred into one of Brewster's legitimate accounts right here in the city.

Any transaction over 10k sets off a red flag with the

bank and has to be reported to the IRS and investigated, which a savvy businessman like Brewster would know, of course. So it couldn't be an amateur move on his part; it had to be a failsafe set up by Ericson in the event of his untimely demise.

I didn't have to do too much backtracking and overriding of Ericson's accounts. He was already stealing money from his client. I just had to make it more obvious.

So when the lead detective on the case was alerted of the banking activity surrounding one of his suspects, it didn't take long for a warrant to be issued and a search of Brewster's penthouse to be underway, where the murder weapon was retrieved.

That concludes round one.

I turn on the widescreen in my loft office and flip through local channels. An action so mundane feels foreign to me, the simple act of staring at the TV screen ratchets my anxiety, as if precious time is being wasted.

This could be the result of running on pure adrenaline for the past ninety-six hours—or the fact I have to make a crucial decision soon.

I stop on a news station and force myself to sit. And watch.

For round two:

The second and hardest part of the scheme was actually getting my switchblade with Ericson's DNA into Brewster's penthouse at The Plaza. The high price tag on the attic unit ensures the best security measures, and I couldn't just walk the weapon in myself and plant it.

I had to have one of Brewster's thugs walk it in. Fortunately, my weeks spent stalking Ericson during his revenge job coincided with Brewster's crew's schedule. I knew of at least three gentlemen's clubs where his guys liked to frequent.

I hesitated a moment before I wiped the knife hilt clean of my prints, then one sexy and meticulous lap dance with the right thug placed the switchblade in a briefcase that was soon on its way to the penthouse. Just in time for the two-day search of Brewster's penthouse and financials.

Once the connection to Ericson's murder was made, the detectives had an easier time linking the other victims to Brewster via their bank records and metadata.

Records and metadata I fabricated.

Like Reilly Stafford, who had a known drug habit. Reilly paid for his supply by middle-manning one of Brewster's college drug rings. And Caleb Foster, a financial adviser at another firm who Ericson placed in charge of one of Brewster's offshore accounts. And Christopher Monroe, an owner of a high-end car dealership that Brewster used to launder money through. And the dealership's adviser? One Ericson Daverns.

Which looks something like this: Ericson was stealing a gross amount of money from his client, giving

Brewster motive to have Ericson killed. The other murders were cleanup on Brewster's end, to make sure any questionable connections between Ericson and Brewster were removed.

If this was one of my revenge jobs, I would have titled it Ring Around the Gangster.

Maybe I would've come up with something better back then. My sense of humor has taken a hit since the inception of my emotions.

Although, according to Vanessa, she prefers the more delicate and expressive version of her daughter. As Vanessa Vaughn will not be ran out of her city, she refused to leave when I pleaded with her. So instead, I kept a close watch over her, which included a dinner that saved a lot of unnecessary money flying toward legal teams. All I had to do was convince her *her way* was what was best for me, and take her advice.

I promised her my lawyer had convinced me to lay low until the investigation was over. I looked her right in her eyes—the hard green gems that mirror my own—and admitted what happened in the alleyway was self-defense, that I was finally coming to terms with the truth.

After I agreed to see her therapist, all was right again in the world of socialites and their murderous offspring.

It seems that's all a mother truly wants, for her child to be safe and…happy.

Strange, all these years with uncomfortable discord between us, and all I had to do was take some random guidance from my mother and let her see how grateful I was.

Becoming closer with my mother was, honestly, the strangest part of this whole nightmare. Don stripper gear and give a lap dance to a gangster? No problem. Have dinner with my mother and tell her *thank you*? The world tilts off its axis.

The newswoman on screen grabs my attention as Brewster's name appears on the caption. I click the button to unmute the television.

"Today an arrest was made of one of the city's most notorious playboys and philanthropists. Shane Brewster was charged in the murder of chief financial adviser, Ericson Daverns. Brewster is also being indicted on several counts of racketeering, bribery, and money laundering, as well as charges of organized drug sales."

I click off the TV.

The shopping list of charges the DA is tacking onto Brewster's prosecution is simply to make sure he goes down for something, while getting the max time.

Brewster can get out of a murder charge. He'll pin it on one of his guys to take the fall. It's the money he can't—ironically—buy his way out of.

The government wants their tax dollars.

As the pieces fall into place, a sense of justified rightness settles over me. I was never in the revenge game for justice, no matter what Alex claims. My business was self-serving.

Yes, I was cruel.

I had a sickness inside me.

I feared the day that sickness devoured the last dregs of my humanity and I became a real monster.

But it was always that fear, that awareness of my nature, which kept me inline and the consuming darkness at bay. It was always in my power. Even as a psychopath, I harbored fear of myself.

I lost control when my emotions owned me.

You don't have to be a psychopath to do horrible things—succumbing to our fears can turn us villainous.

Emotions or not, Alex was right, I am the same person.

The heightened sense of thrill courses my veins, almost bringing me to tears. I no longer feel lost, alone. Aimless. Blakely was inside me the whole time, just waiting for me to find her.

I grab my bag and phone as I head to the door.

When I was sitting across from her, London told me that, as long as I was successful in handling Alex, then Grayson had no need to intervene.

She wasn't giving me her assessment of her patient; she was giving me a warning.

When Alex made the threat that London could have me institutionalized, he hinted to a very crucial aspect of the duo's relationship. She's the one in control. She wields the power.

London is the key.

Alex made a deal with Grayson, but I can make a deal with her.

I make the call.

When she answers, I say, "It's done."

A pause fills the line before she replies. "Hello, Blakely. I'm so glad you decided to finally reach out to me."

I walk around a food cart, the pungent scent of overcooked street meat smacking me in the face, and it's still a more favorable greeting than London's.

"The situation has been handled," I say to her, keeping the conversation short and on point. "Alex is out of the picture. I took care of him. I was *successful*." I stress the word to reiterate our conversation.

Silence stretches across the line, then: "What are you going to do now?"

Paused at a crosswalk, I hold up the microchip and squint at the numbers too tiny to discern with the naked eye. "I don't know, honestly. I was thinking about retiring from my current profession, but—" I snap a quick picture of the chip and text it to her number "—first, I might see if this serial number matches any metadata connected to Brewster's case. You know, just in case forensics overlooked anything."

My threat is very clear.

Grayson isn't off the hook yet, and neither is she. The DA could make a very creative case for how a serial killer and his psychologist aided Brewster in eliminating his shady connections.

Here is our ultimate *quid pro quo*.

As long as we each have something or some*one* to lose, we can reach an agreement.

"I think that's unnecessary," London finally says. "I'm sure the authorities have everything they need to make their case."

Checkmate.

"I'm moving out of the country," she continues. "It's a shame we didn't get to have another session before I fly out. I truly wanted to help you solve your dilemma. Of course, I can always analyze the data remotely, send you my findings."

My phone vibrates, and I lower the device to open a text. A picture of a USB drive—Alex's USB drive—appears on the screen.

A humorless laugh festers inside me. London is keeping the status quo for damn sure.

Alex admitted he can't recreate the treatment. He's failed with three subjects since me. The terrifying truth may be that he even failed with me.

My dilemma is whether or not Alex's torture treatment is the reason my neural pathways altered, or if my feelings for him proves I'm a disempathetic type, what London brought to my attention during our meeting.

This is why Grayson stole Alex's formula. London wants to conduct her own research into the cure of psychopaths.

And I was going to be her control, her basis for comparison.

Alex was absolutely right. Had I not found a way to threaten the couple, then I'd probably be in the back of Grayson's trunk right now, and Alex would be buried at Devil's Peak.

I clamp my hand around the chip, keeping my eyes on the crossing sign as it signals to walk. I don't move. Car horns blare and people pass in a hurry on foot and bikes, and I stand stalled on the sidewalk.

"I appreciate your concern," I say, "but I'm not interested in any further research."

Breath bated, I wait to hear her response.

"I understand. Thank you for your help securing loose ends." London's voice sounds faraway in my ear. "Have a nice life, Blakely Vaughn."

She ends the call.

A *whoosh* of air escapes my lungs.

So that's it. I get to walk away as no one's lab rat, and Alex gets to live.

It's over. I have to accept this is an element out of my control. Alex lost his research, but we're alive. We're free to decide what we do with our life.

A tradeoff I can for damn sure live with.

Glancing around the busy intersection, I stand at the corner of the crosswalk. There's a fork before me, two directions to choose from.

My very first choice to make.

One direction leads to the kennel. The other leads out of the city, away from Alex.

I could disappear right now. Walk away from Alex and this whole sordid life.

But even as I'm debating my choice, my feet move in a familiar direction.

I reach the kennel and push the key into the door. As I walk into the front, the silence thrums my nerves. I glance around for Addisyn. She's not supposed to leave Alex alone. Ever.

Irritation twists my stomach, but, in truth, I never trusted a dog crate to hold Alex. I knew there was a better than slim chance he'd escape, but I just needed a head start.

"Addisyn," I call out. "You psycho nut, the deal was you weren't supposed to leave."

As I enter the back, everything appears the same as it did four days ago.

A sliver of relief uncoils the tension in my muscles. I take a single moment to process what I'm about to do, then I step toward the cage. Alex is there, wearing the same clothes and looking a little more haggard. Keeping his back to me, he won't turn around. He won't look at me.

A charge fills the air the closer I get. He could've escaped—but he didn't. Which means he chose to let me do this my way. He also trusted that I'd come back for him. Whether he's full-on delusional, I guess it no longer matters.

The small span of distance between us is eaten as I move toward the cage.

I dig the key out of my pocket and push it into the lock.

"Yeah, I'm stunned stupid too that I'm actually here—" But as the words leave my mouth, I notice the tension on the padlock.

Only it's too late.

I hear a *click*, then a loud whirring noise. The top of the cage is yanked backward as the sides fall away. Alex's arms are stretched above his head as he's hoisted into the air, suspended before me.

Oh, my god.

A trap has been triggered.

I called checkmate too soon.

INERTIA

ALEX

*I*n physics, inertia is the consistency of force moving at the same speed, on the same path, without change, unless interrupted.

In life, inertia is a state of apathy, lethargy. Idleness. The state of remaining the same, unmoved and unmovable.

Before Blakely, I never thought of life outside of science. Everything had a scientific explanation. And I was on a course to greatness, even if the world would never appreciate my discovery, my sacrifice. My ego was so that I didn't sense my inertia, how I was drifting on a linear path, stagnant, for an unmeasurable timeframe.

I could've existed in that dormant state forever.

Until she interrupted my state of being.

The most unfeeling and cruel creature—inhumane by her own design—crashed my world of metrics and careful calculations and changed me. With a darkly ironic twist, she made me see the world through a human lens.

So as I'm thrust into the air, my wrists and ankles bound by cable, my limbs stretched and my body racked, all I can see is how astonishingly beautiful she is below me. How the widening of her sea-green eyes convey her vortex of emotions. How her parted mouth, her words hung in suspension just as I am, begs to be kissed to steal away her fear.

She removes all doubt.

"Alex—" she shouts, spinning in a circle below me. "What the fuck is going on?"

The cables cinch tighter, slicing into my skin, and I grit out a response. "You need to leave. Now, Blakely. Go—"

Even as I glut the painful words from the bowels of my desire to keep her, I know it's already too late.

The timepiece starts to descend from the joist in the middle of the room, the ticking amplified by the speaker and acoustics. I watched Grayson design majority of the trap, but he left me in the dark for his finale.

When she left me in this cage, I knew where Blakely would start. I figured I'd give her a day to ease into her scheme before I picked the lock and took care of Addisyn who, by the way, spent most of her time on her phone and complaining of boredom, while she paid little notice to me.

I should have acted sooner.

I should have been more thorough.

But as always, when it comes to Blakely, I'm too narrowly focused on her to foresee the variables.

During our three days together, Grayson enlightened me on a number of details. The Rolex he stitched into my leg wasn't a warped countdown measure; it was to conceal the tracker he placed beneath my skin.

Brilliant, really, because the painful wound masked any discomfort the tiny tracking device might have caused.

Grayson's curiosity was piqued when the GPS dot showed me spending a great deal of time at a dog kennel. Oh, he had a laugh, walking in to discover me caged like an animal by the torturous love of my life.

"In love, we are all trapped," I said to him.

"Indeed," was his reply.

I spent the next seventy-two hours torn between my selfish need for Blakely to return, and my hope she wouldn't—that she'd run away and, this time, she'd never look back.

Blakely stares at my pocket watch dangling from the beam as if she's been entranced by the rhythmic ticking. When she finally speaks, her voice is low and monotone. "I kept the bargain," she says, her gaze flicking up to find mine. "Brewster is handled. All the murders are pinned on him and his crew. Grayson is in the clear." She wipes a hand across her forehead in thought. "I kept the fucking deal."

"But the deal wasn't with you."

Grayson leans against the back wall, arms crossed over his chest. He's partially obscured by the shadows in the room, his light gaze assessing first Blakely, then me.

He cocks an eyebrow. "I'm surprised the trap worked," he says, his admission unexpected. "I had limited supplies to work with here."

After he drugged Addisyn with the animal sedatives, he rigged a medieval stretching device using the top of the crate as a rack. The suspension is geared by a simple cable hoist. If not for my extremely uncomfortable predicament, I'd appreciate the mechanics.

He's not as smug as I first perceived him. With an IQ to rival my own, he views the world like one giant puzzle he's always piecing together, as evident with his meticulous traps. Admittedly, he has a very macabre picture in mind of that completed puzzle, but at this point in my life, strung from cables like a morbid marionette, I'm not one to judge.

"Your trap is unnecessary," Blakely says, her voice rising over her fear. "Like I said, I took care of

Brewster. The investigation into the murders is over. None of it is a threat to you, or to London."

Grayson's eyes flare at the mention of his psychologist.

A tense silence chokes the air as the two of them stay locked in a stare off, some measure of threat passing between them.

Not for the first time, I wish I was privy to that first conversation between Blakely and London. If only she had let me in completely, we might have been able to beat the disturbed duo at our own game instead of playing theirs.

Grayson is the first to break the spell. The corner of his mouth hitches with the faintest smile. "We had a bet on whether or not you'd show, whether you'd leave Alex here to rot."

I grunt as the cables bite into my bones, cutting off circulation. "She showed," I say.

Blakely glances up at me. "Did you bet I'd come or not?"

That's a loaded question. Grayson releases a chuckle. "Yes, Chambers, do you call this a win?"

"You can let her go," is all I say. There was no negotiating for my life, so I wagered Blakely's. Not that I trust the honor code of the man who rammed an icepick through my sister's brain—but it was my only option to try to protect her.

I expel a strained breath, a tangled fusion of regret

and relief tightening my chest. I want Blakely out of danger, but I also want to believe what tethers us together is stronger than a successful treatment and her malice toward me.

Yes, greedily, I wanted her to come for me.

Grayson pushes off the wall and takes unhurried steps toward the pocket watch. "I am a man of my word," he says to her. "You're free to go, Blakely."

She licks her lips, stalling. "And what happens to Alex?"

Standing in the middle of the room, he touches the pocket watch, giving it a spin. "Do you care?"

She's silent a beat before she says, "If you're a man of your word, then you have to release him. You got what you initially asked for—"

"You're trying to debate with a psychopath," I interrupt. "Think, Blakely. There was never any real deal. His methodology is full of loopholes. It was always going to end this way. Grayson just likes to toy with his victims first."

We discussed this. I told her we had no choice. When I tried to convince her to help me murder Grayson and Brewster, turning her into a full-fledged killer. The idea seems so preposterous now, how I believed I had designed her mind to accommodate her revenge skills.

That's not why she stabbed Ericson.

His murder wasn't done out of justice or revenge or

even her uncontrollable emotions—it was to protect an innocent life.

She was never the monster.

I was.

"That's why you need to go," I say, starting to feel lightheaded as I answer my own internal monologuing. "Let me make it right."

Grayson watches her closely, regarding her with a curious look. At her intense silence, Grayson nods knowingly.

Blakely drops her bag to the floor, her declaration voiced in one action.

"Regardless of loopholes," Grayson says, "releasing Alex isn't my call to make. It's yours, Blakely."

She lifts her chin in defiance, and my heart batters my rib cage. "What is the trap?" she demands.

My eyes close briefly in defeat. She's going to play his game.

"I was impressed with your design for the trap," Grayson says to her, moving toward the grooming area. "A very simple yet precise design around your victim, using Alex's own pocket watch to lure him into the cage. I respect the personal touch. I admired it so much, in fact, I decided to utilize it myself. With a few minor alterations."

He shoves a white partition aside to reveal what's behind the panel.

Blakely steps forward, then stops, rethinking her response. She's not used to acting on impulse.

Addisyn is strapped to a gurney, much like the one I used on my subjects, like the one I was restrained to while Grayson tried to cook my brain. She's tipped into an upright position, her mouth gagged. Her eyes blink furiously as she struggles against the straps.

Grayson pulls out a phone from his back pocket and taps the screen.

Blakely's phone vibrates with a text. As she reads the message, I can see her making the full connection. She's been communicating with Grayson for the past few days, not Addisyn. While I've been pissing and shitting on a dog toilet, drinking out of a water bowl and being fed dog treats by a serial killer, I wasn't sure what happened to the woman Blakely left in charge.

Admittedly, I assumed he killed her. But that would go against his fucked-up moral code, I suppose.

My biceps are starting to burn, my back aches from pressing into the mesh grating. I attempt to reposition myself, and the cables band tighter around my wrists.

Whatever Grayson ultimately wants, it won't come without a price—a price that will be too steep for either of us to pay.

We're not leaving here unscathed, unchanged, even if we manage to live.

Grayson watches me as I watch Blakely, getting some sick satisfaction out of my misery. She looks up from her phone, her face pale and all traces of confusion removed from her delicate features.

"What else do I have to do?" Blakely asks Grayson, her tone now hesitant, having lost some of its edge.

With an excited gleam in his eyes, Grayson removes a vial from his pocket and places it on the counter, then deposits a second vial right next to it. I squint at the bottles, like I can actually read the labels without my glasses.

After a lengthy beat, where he holds Blakely's gaze, he says, "Sometimes, we don't know what we want, or even understand who we are, until we're forced to confront our darkest fears. Choice opens our eyes."

She lowers her phone and glares across the room at him. "So, this is all for my benefit?" She releases a tense, mocking laugh. "Well fuck, am I supposed to thank you?"

"Actually," he says, removing a box of disposable gloves from a cabinet and slipping a pair on, "you can thank London. She's invested in your awakening, as she refers to it. I'm just the instrument."

"What is he talking about?" I ask Blakely, but she doesn't respond. She's studying Grayson with guarded apprehension and acute focus.

Suddenly, I realize none of this—framing Brewster; the subjects I killed linking to Grayson—was about me. This is between Blakely and London.

"But more than anything," Grayson says, "I'm

selfish. This is my assurance that every single loose thread is knotted nice and tight. I hate those sloppy loose ends."

He produces a third vial and a cotton swab. As he breaks eye contact with Blakely to step toward Addisyn, alarm lights up every nerve in my body. Grayson submerges the swab in the liquid contents of the vial, being extremely cautious not to drip any, his movements slow and precise. A tight band of terror coils my spine.

"It's a toxin," I say, my mouth dry and voice gruff. "Blakely, go. Now. Get out!"

She remains where she is, refusing to move or react, or to even look at me. What the hell did his text say to her?

A furious whip of anger lashes my insides. I try to kick out of the restraints, but only manage to snap the fucking cables tighter. Every time I struggle, the hoist turns a cog, and I'm racked and stretched. My muscles are on fire. Phantom flames lick the scar tissue of my hand. And I watch, petrified, as Grayson dabs the cotton tip across Addisyn's sweat-slicked collarbone as she squirms, her cry muffled by the gag.

"Actually, it's a nerve agent," Grayson corrects me. He holds the saturated cotton swab a safe distance from his body. "One of the deadliest nerve agents engineered by man."

XV, I think, as my pulse thuds against my neck. "That's not possible," I say, although I know it wouldn't be *im*possible for me to engineer the compound myself —but how the hell would Grayson have access to those chemicals?

Instead of acknowledging my statement, Grayson turns in my direction. "I really appreciate Mary's inscription to you. While I was repairing the watch, I kept reading it, and it finally clicked why you have such an obsession with clocks."

"Fuck you," I say, keeping his attention trained on me and away from Blakely. "You don't know anything about me."

"Alex, I created you," he says, false pride lacing his deep voice. "*Our cerebral death gives way to our rebirth.* That's how you cited it. *A necrosis of the mind.* You stated it in your journal yourself, and I'm agreeing with you. Because I killed what made you human when I took your sister's life, you're a product of my design." He tilts his head. "Very lyrical for a man of science."

I grit my teeth, jaw clenched to the point of pain. "It was a metaphor, you twisted fuck."

"I don't buy that." His smile doesn't meet his callous eyes. "But regardless, I do know what makes you *tick*, Chambers."

A low chuckle escapes. "Always the narcissist, to assume that passage was written about you," I say, accepting where this is heading. "*She* is the reason."

Something flashes behind his darkened gaze. "Let's test a theory."

As Grayson approaches me with the swab, Blakely finally reacts. She lunges at him too late for me to warn her, my shout crackling against my eardrums. If one particle of that swab comes into contact with her skin, there will be nothing I can do to save her.

Even as she manages to strike Grayson, nailing him with a hard jab to his face, it's already over. It's done.

I feel the damp cotton graze my skin.

The event progresses as if in slow motion. Grayson touches his smarting cheek as he smiles and reaches out. Her gaze follows his hand as he makes contact with my leg, her eyes trailing upward as he moves out of her reach. She's poised there, calm as our river, my force of wrath and vengeance, with nowhere to deliver her retribution.

When her eyes drift up to reach mine, a moment of pure mayhem passes between us, everything said and unsaid. There's no going backward. Time doesn't reverse. It won't stand still.

The seconds keep slipping away.

I knew it would never end in a beautiful embrace. But I thought, with all my goddamn intelligence, it wouldn't end so unsatisfactory, so wasteful. All the years ahead, every calculation I did to measure the time left on this planet...I'm a fucking asshole.

"Stop your inner monologuing, Chambers," Grayson interrupts my thoughts, snapping his fingers to get my attention.

I blink a few times, wondering if the nerve agent is already causing hazard to my system. How long do I have before my brain deteriorates?

Blakely steps away from Grayson and takes out her phone, keeping her gaze level on him. "How long?" she demands, echoing my fear.

He lifts his chin. "By the time help arrives, he'll be dead. He's dead already. They both are." He ticks his head in the direction of Addisyn. "If you call for help, you'll just burden yourself with the obligation of trying to explain why there's a dead body with a nerve agent in the blood."

Thumb hovering over the Call button, Blakely narrows her gaze. "*A* dead body."

I'm still mentally aware enough to catch the deliberate slip, and I look at the counter, to where Grayson set the two other vials.

After he discards the swab and bottle, along with his gloves, in the trash bin, he walks to the middle of the room and reaches up to flip the pocket watch around. "Perfect timing." A slow smile stretches his lips. "Alex wrote so much about you in his journal, Blakely. You have a thing for bullies. They get under your skin. Addisyn is a bully, and Alex is a bully," he points out.

Blakely shakes her head, her blond tresses bouncing along her shoulders in the way that always makes my chest ache. "Just answer the fucking question."

I might be feeling the effects of the nerve agent

already, or it could be psychosomatic. But I want my last vision as I leave consciousness to be of her.

Impatience gathers Blakely's hands into fists as she makes for the vials, coming to the same deduction as me.

The antidote to the XV nerve agent is a combination of Atropine and pralidoxime chloride administered in a very specific dosage, delivered at specific intervals until the effects have subsided.

And it's possibly residing in those glass bottles.

"You can choose only one to save," Grayson says, halting Blakely's steps. "There's not enough antidote for two. But seriously, killing them both would save you a lot of trouble."

"I'm not killing anyone. You are," she retorts.

"You made a choice to kill this girl   " he motions to Addisyn "—the moment you used her for your selfish endeavor. Remember, honesty is your only course here."

Blakely nails Grayson with a deadly glare. "How. Fucking. *Long*?"

Grayson leisurely heads toward the double doors. "Ten minutes," he finally answers. "Maybe fifteen, before the symptoms present. And they are gruesome. But by then, it will be too late."

"You're a savage," Blakely says to him, her voice laced with venom.

He grabs a strip of bandage. "I can cover their eyes with this—" he looks at the neon strip that reads: *Give me treats*—"doggy bandage. It is easier when you don't have to look your victims in the eyes."

Ignoring his chiding remark, Blakely proceeds to grab the vials. As she turns around to look for Grayson, he's already gone.

"Fuck," she hisses. "What is the dosage?" Her gaze wanders to me, and yes, I know the proper dosage.

But that's not what she really wants to know.

I wish this was my choice to make—it's an easy one for me.

I'd choose her. I will always choose her.

But that's precisely why this isn't my choice to make.

The activity of the city hums outside these walls. The flurry of life, the night an orchestra, the world minding its own business, as we're trapped in a pit with our darkest thoughts.

The ticking of my pocket watch grows louder as I remain racked and suspended.

Blakely stands center of the room, hands clutched to the vials and syringe, her despondent gaze locked on me.

"Think of it as *coup de grâce*." I offer a weak smile. "This time, you have no choice, Blakely. Give me my mercy killing."

This is my chance to rewrite our script. The villain gets his redemptive ending.

BURN ME TWICE

BLAKELY

J've been here before.

Only this time, even though the flames are figurative, they burn twice as hot.

Alex had asked me to kill him in the dark room, when he placed a river stone in my hand. His demons were torturing him, and to quiet them, to put a permanent stop to his madness and the killing, I knew what I had to do.

But I was too weak, and I consciously allowed the fire to make the choice for me.

Was my weakness due to crippling emotions? Because I had never experienced love before?

I still don't fully understand, but as the seconds tick

around us on an endless, echoing loop, I drop Alex's gaze and light my phone screen, reading over Grayson's text to try to glean a different meaning.

You and I are very similar, Blakely, the only difference is, you were born, where I was made. The psychopathic mind cannot be altered. I think, in time, you'll find yourself regressing to your former baseline self, where your emotions resort to shallow affect—all except for one unavoidable aspect: your feelings for Alex. This is the strange anomaly. Love can remake us, again and again, we are reborn. If you're honest with yourself, then the rest will unravel effortlessly. The only way out of this trap is to accept who you are, and embrace the darkness you were born with.

I toss the phone, letting it clatter loudly to the tile floor.

I couldn't kill Alex then, and God help me, I can't kill him now.

I'm fated to my weakness, the same as Alex's fate has always been time.

Time will take him before I can.

I tuck the vials into my jeans and hold on to the syringe as I rush to the hoist contraption. Muttering a curse, I make a snap judgment to pull the rusted lever, and the *zip* of the cable line races across my skin, making me shiver.

Alex collapses to the floor.

"Shit, sorry." I grab up the cable and follow it until I

reach him, where I untwist one end from around his wrist, then the other.

He says nothing as he tips his head back and brings his palm to my face. The bandage is missing. His scars are rough against my skin. He's shaking due to the abuse to his muscles. As his pale-blue eyes capture mine, I stop moving, stop breathing.

"How are you feeling?" I ask.

He licks his lips. "I'm not sure. Maybe it will hit all at once, be quick."

My chest pangs with a hollow ache. I swallow the fiery lump in my throat, then take a moment to glance at Addisyn. She's still breathing. Calm. No signs of symptoms yet.

"Here," Alex says, as he removes the syringe from my hand. He uses his thumb to measure out each dose I'll need to administer along the barrel. "Give her a dose of each every five minutes until the effects subside."

My heart batters my chest wall, making it difficult to breathe. I look at the watch strung from the rafter. Four minutes have already passed. Time is slipping through my fingers.

I meet Alex's eyes and, with a trembling hand, brush his hair away from his forehead. "I don't have a choice," I say, a flame licking my lungs.

"I know," he says. "This is the only choice you can make. I don't think I'm capable of being the man who deserves you. I'm too greedy. I'll hurt and maim and kill to keep you, and will feel no regret. I'll never stop, Blakely."

His mouth tips into that endearing, boyish smile—the one that first made me notice how beautiful he was, and also made me loathe him. I think I knew from the start that, if only I was capable, I could fall for Alex.

But we became too dark, too twisted, and I don't know how to move past all the pain and damage we've caused...especially to each other.

London says *awakening*. Grayson claims *rebirth*. Alex believes necrosis can kill enough brain cells to alter us, as if it's as simple as letting a piece of me die. The piece I'd have to sacrifice is the one which has kept my moral sense on track, even when I had no empathy to guide me.

My conscience.

I'm not sure what would be born in its place. How could I trust that Alex and I wouldn't fall so far down the rabbit hole we'd be lost forever?

We'd have each other.

A goddamn tear slips down my cheek, and Alex gathers it with his thumb.

"Ask me to kiss you," he says.

Leave it up to this twisted asshole to get his way on his fucking death bed.

My lips quiver as I lean into him and whisper across his lips. "Kiss me, Alex."

He grasps the back of my neck and brings my mouth

to his. His lips are soft but firm, conveying the torn emotions thrumming through the both of us. The kiss starts as a slow simmer, then he infuses it with blistering heat, building into a passionate fire destined to consume. I'm left breathless as I match his intensity.

Suddenly, he stills and, as I pull away, I read the shock in his widening eyes. I move back so he can sit forward, his gaze dropping between us to where the needle punctures his arm. The empty syringe rests in my hand, my thumb depressing the plunger.

As his gaze lifts, his features draw together in confusion. "Blakely?"

My name asks every question, demands every answer.

"Because I don't have a choice," I admit to him. I touch his face gently, trying to detect if the antidote is working. "Because I love you. And I'm too selfish to let you go."

The sickness within me refuses to lose him. It dominates rationality, my conscience—even my sense of justice, where I still crave revenge on Alex. All of it pales to my need to keep him with me.

As Alex stares at me in wonder, some other desperate emotion passes across his face, and he again looks down at the syringe.

"What is it?" I ask. My heartbeat flutters erratically in my pulse.

He removes the needle and holds up the barrel,

analyzing the remainder of the contents. "It's clear," he says, as if answering some internal question. He pushes a drop of fluid onto his finger and tastes it.

At his prolonged silence, I drag in a breath, impatience striking my nerves like flint. "Alex…?"

"It's water."

My heart drops, my lungs clawing for air as an icy sensation trickles through my veins, leaving me cold. "He tricked us…lied to us?" But even as I voice my fears aloud, I know it's pointless.

Grayson likes to toy with his victims.

Alex said this would end bloody.

I start to stand, to do…something, *anything*. Call for help. Call London and scream—but Alex grabs my hand, preventing me from caving into panic.

"There are no symptoms," he says, trying to reach me. "I don't have any symptoms, and it's been—" he glances at his pocket watch "—but I still can't see that far."

As adrenaline crests, I tear my hand free and look at the time. "Eleven minutes."

Realization slices deep, and I search for the phone. I'm typing a text to Grayson as I see three little dots appear. I wait with bated breath for his message.

It's exceedingly ridiculous, don't you think, that I'd have access to a military-grade nerve agent? Really, I gave Alex far more credit. But sometimes, you don't need to be extreme to get extreme results.

"Fuck." I drop the phone in my lap and wipe my hands down my face, a fierce mix of anger and relief tearing through my nervous system.

I feel Alex's touch as he brings me back from the brink. Then he stands and limps to the trash bin, where he digs out the vial Grayson tossed, confirming the contents are also water.

A manic laugh springs free, and I glance at Addisyn, who is mumbling something frantic beneath her gag. Maybe I should release her and let her in on the full outcome, but she's still a despicable human being, and a few more minutes won't literally kill her.

My phone vibrates in my lap, sending a spike of apprehension careening through me. Warily, I turn the screen over.

Loose ends…they're a threat that just won't go away. They have to be cut off so they don't fray out of control. I'd like to assume I know the choice you made, and if I'm right, then you've already made the hardest decision of all. What you have to do next will be relatively easy.

The world needs people like us, Blakely. It needs us to weed the vilest subhumans from existence to balance humanity. Don't fall victim to the weak mindset that held you back for so long. Addisyn is what a true monster looks like. Your research didn't uncover all her secrets.

The choice is still yours, of course, but it would be highly unwise to disappoint me.

Look in the drawer.

PS – London says "hello." Oh, and not to worry about digging up the earth at Devil's Peak. All has been relocated for you.

This time, when I throw the phone, I make sure it breaks. The screen cracks on impact, going dark.

All has been relocated. All—as in the remains of Alex's subjects.

If we walk away right now, Alex never has to know what the message said. I can let Addisyn go and threaten her to leave the city. I can force her to disappear. Then we can disappear, too.

"I'll do it."

Alex's sure voice breaks into my thoughts, and I turn to see him standing behind me, his body bearing the pain from being racked, but strong in the way only Alex can be. With absolute, sheer conviction.

"I guess you can make an educated guess as to what he wants," I say.

As he moves toward me, his eyes holding mine with resolve, he says, "You'll despise me for doing it, but he's not wrong. It has to be done. I'll do it, so you don't have to."

He wants to spare me the guilt. I mean, for him, what's one more body to add to the count? If only that was the matter tearing me apart.

I gave too much away to London, and she used every single scrap against me, against us.

If we don't get rid of Addisyn, if we give the diabolical duo any reason at all to come after us, those bones from Devil's Peak will resurface somewhere, and it won't be Alex's sister who is splashed across the news and social media.

There will be a manhunt.

For Alex.

How can I save his life and not...*save his life*?

Anger courses my blood like molten shards as I stalk to the counter and open the drawers one-by-one until I find the hunting knife Grayson left behind. I want to rage over the fact I was manipulated. But really, in the back of my mind, a tiny voice whispers a taunt.

Grayson made it easier for me.

By forcing me to first choose between Alex and Addisyn's life with the mock nerve agent, the choice to now kill Addisyn doesn't feel as consequential. Just five minutes ago, she was dead already. And allowing Alex to kill Addisyn seems like an insignificant price to pay to keep our secrets.

Grayson won't know who did the deed.

All that matters is his fucking *loose ends* are no longer a threat.

Besides, I have no excuses left. I asked for this torture when I threatened London with the microchip, didn't I? No, further back...when I tipped the first domino by sending her that email.

TRISHA WOLFE

I wrap my hand around the knife hilt and shut my eyes against the building pressure.

My temples throb, a residual side-effect from electroshock. High anxiety triggers the reaction, as if my body is reminded of what it has endured. I almost laugh as I test the weight of the hunting knife. I'm so full of shit.

Just a few days ago, I was plotting Alex's demise. I was hate-fucking him in a skywalk bathroom. Now I'm mentally torturing myself over removing one of my targets? A sadistic homewrecker? How many other women would secretly choose to end Addisyn's life if there was no judgment, no consequences? If the rules didn't apply to them?

This isn't about her, or these fucking emotions, or the guilt. I knew what I was capable of the moment I shoved a little boy's face in an ant bed.

Who I am—my true nature—was inescapable.

"Blakely." Alex's voice comes from behind me, a summons.

I close the drawer and turn toward him, the knife held before me. A worried divot creases the space between his eyebrows, and I step forward and smooth the wrinkle away with my thumb, then palm his face, letting the abrasive feel of his shadowed stubble comfort me.

He's so familiar…

I slip the handle of the knife into his palm.

278

"This will be over soon," he assures me.

I nod, even though we both know that's a lie we're telling ourselves.

This won't ever be over.

This is only the start.

Alex places a tender kiss to my forehead before he turns and starts in the direction of Addisyn.

My heart knocks painfully in my chest, adrenaline climbing. I watch as he stops right in front of her, knife cast down near his thigh. He stares into her eyes—eyes wide with fear, her cheeks blotchy and wet from tears.

As Alex rests the blade above her collarbone, I can hardly hear her high-pitched squeal over the roaring of my heart. I swear the muscle is either going to burst or stop beating.

I'm becoming lightheaded, as if I'm watching from outside myself. I've never experienced such an intense rush.

I can't claim what emotion is rioting through me, maybe all of them. Like Alex's black room, the darkest color in existence being a mixture of all colors, my soul is darkening with every emotion.

The sensation grips me, owning me before I can master control of my thoughts or actions.

I decide it's better if we don't think, when letting a piece of ourselves die.

As I move in close to stand beside Alex, I breathe in the remnants of his faded cologne, and the undercurrent sears my veins. His body heat singes my skin, thrilling. Then I see my hand slip along his forearm as I coast down to place my hand over his.

His heavy breaths rend the air, and I sense each one as if he's breathing through me, into me. We stay suspended like this—the knife held to her neck; a nick of blood staining the tip—our hands locked together, until he says the one thing he can't take back.

"Together."

I rest my cheek against his arm, feeling the strain of his muscles. "Together."

I'm not sure which one of us initiates the kill, but we move in tandem, the drag of the blade across her skin echos through us. Applying more force, we push the knife deeper until we feel the steel hit bone. Once we pass the artery, the gurgling sound muffles her moans.

I lace my fingers through his as the flow of red covers our hands.

I don't look away—I stare into her desolate eyes as she begins to fade, her lids fluttering as she fights to stay conscious. I'm surprised by the numbness. Then suddenly that dull, hazy gray dissipates, and a bloom of colors unfold. So vibrant.

Alex removes the knife as her head lulls forward, but he doesn't release my hand. He uses his other hand to cover mine, the warmth a mix of blood and his body heat. All I can do is stare at our blood-coated, entwined fingers.

The same way I stared at my blood-stained palms after I stabbed a man.

Only I was alone then.

I'm not now.

I refused to admit the truth before, but there's no denying it now, not with Alex studying my eyes, knowing what impulses are firing to which synapses in my brain. He can read me, my emotions a simple equation to him.

Keeping our fingers threaded together, he pulls me close. He doesn't say it; he doesn't have to. The intoxicating combination of blood and his heady scent is an aphrodisiac, coaxing me even closer, and I meet him there, our bodies colliding together.

Lust. Comfort. Purging.

We experience it all in a secret chamber of our minds. We express what's too overwhelming to be voiced through desperate caresses and needy kisses, taking and giving and loving until we've expended every energy-carrying molecule between us.

When the heightened emotions start to ebb and release us, we do what's necessary to remain free—to remain together.

EPILOGUE

MALADY

BLAKELY

*M*ary Shelley wrote: "It is true, we shall be monsters, cut off from all the world; but on that account we shall be more attached to one another."

I once referred to Alex as Dr. Victor Frankenstein. With his makeshift mad scientist's lab, and his medieval instruments designed to torture, he was the very essence of the fiendish scientist who sought to create life from death, to make man a god.

Alex viewed my psychopathy as a form of emotional death. To him, I was lifeless, unfeeling, wielding the ability to hurt and cause injury cruelly and without remorse. And like the doctor, he aimed to bring me to life, to give me the capacity to feel, to experience empathy, to suffer guilt.

I was already a monster in his eyes, and he would not only breathe metaphorical life into me, he would recreate me in his image.

What an obvious god complex.

Yet, for all their similarities, none drew a deeper parallel to Shelley's sinister character than Alex subjecting his cruel experiment on the unwilling and taking lives he deemed expendable. In doing so, Alex himself became the monster.

The point of all scientific endeavors is to answer a question, to solve a problem.

Alex claimed psychopaths were the problem, that our ability to kill and cause pain mercilessly needed a solution. But I never believed this, not really.

Having recently experienced the depth of emotions, I discovered what it feels like to be alone, to feel so isolated you can't breathe, you can't function. Loneliness is a disease that will wither your body and mind far more ruthlessly than any physical illness.

Alex was alone.

That was the truth of his incurable malady.

In the novel, the monster demanded that Frankenstein create a soulmate for him to share in his misery, so he would not suffer alone. Even to a gruesome monster, the reality of living his life in solitude was too great to bear.

Alex was a conundrum in that he shared characteristics with both the doctor and the monster simultaneously.

After he lost his twin sister, the last of his family, I'd argue this was the true catalyst for his descent into madness. Not the desire to restore her reputation (though discovering such a horrific secret about one's sibling could nudge one closer to the edge), but it was staring into a lonely future that catapulted the first experiment.

When Alex found me, he wasn't trying to cure a disease, but rather, he wanted to create another monster in his likeness to share in his misery.

Even the most cruel and monstrous villains desire love.

And fiends like Alex and I are in fact detached from the larger world. We had to create an existence of our own, governed by our own logic and rules, an existence we share only with one another.

In my case, it was love that nearly destroyed me. As Victor stated himself through Shelley's narrative: "Nothing is so painful to the human mind as a great and sudden change."

I am a testament to the veracity of that statement.

It's when I stopped fearing change and embraced my evolving nature that I was able to trust my feelings for Alex and accept us together.

As London's advice stated: "You have to learn to embrace your emotions."

She told me this was the only way, and for all her psychotic psychobabble, she was ultimately right when it came to this one crucial element.

The pain and fear and isolation faded into the backdrop of my past, like abstract art splattered on canvas. Disordered, chaotic, frenzied, but the colors bled together to create a beautiful harmony only we can appreciate.

Alex describes it as a closed-loop system coming into alignment. Okay, but I still tend to have a more logical outlook.

Like with what transpired after we took care of Addisyn Meyer.

First, a little backstory:

Grayson was telling the truth in his message; it wasn't a manipulation tactic. My initial research into Addisyn only took me as far as proving she was deserving of my client's revenge. I had no need to dig further, to acquire a toxicology report on Mia's deceased fiancé.

My vetting process was surface level, about as deep as my knowledge of behavior and emotions at the time, where I didn't question why a man, who was trying to rekindle a relationship with his ex-fiancé, would suddenly end his own life. And oddly choose to do so by ingesting acetone—a chemical commonly used by interior decorators to remove paint.

Addisyn was a highly touted interior decorator before I upended her life. Though I can understand why there was never any investigation into his death, and why Addisyn was never suspected in connection.

Honestly, it's a leap. A tenuous connection, at best. Without any evidence, even Mia—who despised Addisyn enough to hire me—never thought Addisyn capable of murder.

Addisyn always wanted what Mia had, though, and if Addisyn couldn't have Mia's man, then she wouldn't let Mia have him either. That was Addisyn's nature.

As I couldn't fathom compassion at the time, I couldn't fit the puzzle pieces together to see the overall picture. I was staring too closely at the abstract image. After reading the tox report, and going through my interview notes with Mia applying my new insight, I was able to take a step back and see what Grayson cleverly deduced.

Addisyn committed murder and made it look like suicide.

Does that condone what Alex and I did?

No. I will never try to justify our actions. Alex and I took her life purely out of selfish need. We ended a life to save our own, to save each other.

But am I suffering guilt over Addisyn?

No. The curious thing about emotions is this: they

allow us to judge from a morally gray perspective that places matters of the heart and our deeper connections and values above banal laws.

I believe most women would mourn the death of a stray dog over the murder of a malicious, murderous homewrecker.

Given the right motivation, we can justify almost anything.

Strangely, as I adapt, I find I was much more law-abiding as a psychopath, when I saw the world in black and white. Having a morally gray outlook has tailored my newest revenge schemes to be much more creative and riskier.

When it came to the cleanup at the kennel, we opted to give Addisyn a proper burial. Well, proper in the regard that we put her in the earth to decompose rather than incinerating the remains to hide the evidence.

Turns out, the best way to dispose of a body is not to dispose of it at all. This is where my logic won out over Alex's mix of science and sentiment. Since Grayson will eventually require proof that we handled the "loose end," we will need access to the body. And since we can't trust the body won't suddenly disappear overnight, we made the choice to stay close.

Besides, it's not as if we could simply pin the murder on our fall guy—not when he was permanently removed from the board.

During our move to Devil's Peak, a report popped

up on my alerts that Shane Brewster died while incarcerated when he asphyxiated in his holding cell. Apparently, Brewster had a very serious shellfish allergy.

Authorities theorized either Brewster couldn't face time on the inside and found a way to off himself, or someone was sent to take him out before he could roll over on a bigger player.

Both are acceptable theories—but here's what Alex and I know: Brewster was a loose end.

After hacking the inmate logs, I confirmed Brewster met with a criminal psychologist for his case. Dr. London Noble made a last-minute stop to conduct a psych eval before she boarded a plane bound for Germany.

Check for the deranged duet.

That makes Alex and I the only remaining loose ends.

Once we arrived at Devil's Peak, with our "cargo" packed in our moving truck, we acquired a timeworn Tudor in foreclosure in the nearest town, then we set to work building a new cottage atop the ruins of Alex's cabin.

We did our due diligence and dug up the earth around the river, confirming the remains of Mary's victims and Alex's subjects had been removed. Then we put Addisyn to rest right there in the ground.

The construction project took ten months. A modern

cottage with all the living necessities, an attached office for my new revenge business, and a detached laboratory for Alex's research.

And then, we waited.

It took another two months before contact was made. A letter arrived at the post office addressed to us right when we were starting to settle into our new life.

Congratulations on your new home and business success. Let's get drinks sometime!

Very short, very puzzling, as Grayson prides himself on being.

We could perceive the letter as a threat. They want us to know they're keeping tabs on us. And after Brewster's unfortunate accident, I doubt I'll ever let London pour me a drink. Or the note could be a hint to London's future plans for the chemical compound she stole from Alex. I'm sure London has questions in need of answers. Or...

Perhaps London and Grayson just have no friends, and this is simply a friendly greeting card. Maybe they really want to stop over for a friendly get-together and then a friendly murder spree.

The fact remains that, whether we're friends, adversaries, nemeses, competition...it's all the same, really. Friends, like enemies, can rarely be trusted, and plotting against the couple helps Alex and I stay ahead of them. Everyone needs a rival, after all. Rivalry keeps us sharp, prevents tedium.

Regardless, we have no choice but to be prepared. We have the word of a methodical serial killer to go on, who, by his own admission, likes to play games.

How do we know the relocated remains won't appear on the news one day simply because the duo become bored and want to spice up their twisted love life?

Since Alex is big on contingency plans, in the event this day comes, we do have a strategy in place. We kept my loft in Tribeca, for one, because Vanessa wouldn't hear of me not maintaining a residence in the city. I stay there when I visit the queen bee.

And for two: Our emergency funds are stashed there. If we ever have to flee the cottage quickly, the loft houses everything we need. Passports. Cash. Suitcases packed with clothes and essentials. A one-hit pit stop to freedom.

I still don't accept the idea of running, but Alex insisted we at least have a backup plan.

I've been more focused on dissecting the details, working out the puzzle. Grayson doesn't do anything without forethought or purpose. I started with the Rolex he embedded in Alex's leg.

Why that pocket watch?

Did he merely pick one up at a pawnshop on his way to torture Alex?

Or does it harbor more significance?

What I found could change the dynamic, altering the status quo.

The antique timepiece was registered with collectables insurance. The value of the watch is in the high four figures. Well, it was, before Grayson welded the chain ribbon, thereby diminishing the value—but the price alone wasn't substantial enough to be the sole reason as to why Grayson chose it.

Simply stated, the watch held meaning.

I was able to trace the owner through the insurance registry, unveiling a whole new twisted maze—one I have no doubt Grayson wants us to wander into, where a trap awaits.

But, I have already followed one white rabbit down a hole, changing my life forever. I'm more than apprehensive to stumble down another. Alice does learn some lessons from Wonderland, after all.

Such as how it wasn't Time's cruelty which trapped the Hatter in a perpetual mad tea party—it was the murder of time which imprisoned him in a punishing loop. Yet, even in a nonsensical realm, the Hatter knew he couldn't beat Time to escape…

Alex didn't.

By smashing his pocket watch and a room full of clocks, Alex deceptively thought he could escape his tormented reality.

That freedom came later, once we bled for each other, after we drew blood for each other.

I can no longer loathe Alex for what he did to me, just as he can no longer loathe my nature.

With the aid of a compound he engineered specifically to help regulate my brain chemistry, in time, my emotions did taper. The overwhelming extremes leveled out, the highs and lows more comparable to the swing of a pendulum. I never returned to my base level of shallow affect, but I also don't suffer the crazy-inducing emotional onslaught, either.

Alex is the only one who takes my feelings to shattering heights.

Our night together under the waterfall did unlock a chamber, some dormant part of my mind, that awoke an emotion strong enough to alter the chemicals of my brain. And despite every rational cell in my body trying to deny it, and in spite of Grayson's claim it can remake us…love is the only possible explanation.

I fell in love with Alex at Devil's Peak.

I fell in love with the devil himself.

And I suppose this rare anomaly makes me disempathetic. A fairy tale psychopath enchanted by her dark Prince Charming.

We are lovesick villains.

My sickness isn't without a form of compassion, however. That is the deciding difference for what governs me from becoming a heartless monster who takes life without thought.

Reason must exist in the face of compassion.

Because without either, I may have killed with the sole purpose of selfish thrill seeking.

We have to accept who we are becoming as the evolution progresses. This rare level of empathy gives me a special ability to select revenge targets who are deserving of not only justice, but of a second chance.

Whereby I design their retribution, and Alex structures their rehabilitation. Though he now refers to his upgraded methods as cognitive aversion restoration.

To me, it's a little derivative of A Clockwork Orange...lacking the fun side effects of the milk. But Alex is improving upon his procedure exponentially, and we now even have one viable test subject.

Some agree to the treatment as a test subject...and some don't. We're very selective with who we vet for each level of our project. Only the vilest, irredeemable human dregs are chosen for the full scope of the treatment without an exit plan.

We discovered a common ground when it came to the continuation of his experiment: London.

Knowing her field of expertise is in rehabilitating dangerous offenders, we expect to see her face appear on social media announcing a breakthrough miracle drug or procedure whereby she'll claim fame to Alex's research.

I don't blame Alex for needing to know if his research and methods would ever result in a cure. Dr.

Frankenstein met his death weighted with regret, wishing he'd killed the monster he created.

Alex isn't seeking atonement; he's pursuing a different fate.

More than support his endeavors to reclaim his research, I have always stood up to bullies. I have never backed down. Thus I refuse to let London call the final *checkmate*.

So for now, the pieces remain unmoved on the board. We cultivate our garden, as quoted by one of Voltaire's great works, by focusing on our projects, on building our life together.

And we wait.

Until it's time to make our move, we explore each other and the intimate world we created. Both the light and dark facets, as they coexist outside of us just as they do within, to be seen, felt, experienced.

What I believe: Every person on this planet has a twisted desire, some sickness and dark hunger begging to be fed. If this wasn't the case, I wouldn't have the lucrative business in revenge that I do.

Whether or not everyone is strong enough to acknowledge their inner monster, well, that's why there are laws, to help the weak keep their devils in check, to make them feel safe and secure in a world that is anything but.

Because there is a little depravity in us all that craves to wander into the darkness.

Some do it safely from the comfort of their homes, investing in entertainment, movies, books.

Others do it more openly, seeking dangerous careers, whether legal or not.

Alex and I accept our twisted malady of the heart. We feed our monsters. We atone in shed blood, locked in each other's arms.

Hell, driven mad, the Hatter tried to drown the dormouse in a teapot. In an alternate world that is completely illogical, murder seems the logical outlet to madness.

Alice spent her whole journey trying to return to her world of logic, where everything made sense, then she awoke only to miss her fantasy.

Draw your parallels to that.

The sound of Alex entering the cottage interrupts my journaling, and I look up from the page to see him lean against the doorway. He's wearing his glasses today, his dark hair disheveled from hours of work. A layer of stubble shadows his jaw.

This is my favorite look on him, especially when his gaze devours me with purposeful intent, all dark yearning and craving reflected in his heated blue eyes.

I tuck my journal away and turn my chair to face him, crossing my legs slowly, seductively, the way I know drives him crazy. "I take it you found something."

Removing his glasses, he pushes off the doorpost and stalks toward me. He drops his glasses on the rustic oak desk before he grabs the armrests of my chair, dragging the desk chair forward and caging me below him.

"Tell me you love me," he says, something devious sparking behind his eyes.

I smile, lick my lips. "I love you, you fucking nut."

Alex groans and captures my face between his palms, crushing his mouth to mine in a feral kiss, stealing my breath and senses.

I slide my hands up his chest, my fingers curling into the worn fabric of his shirt.

When he finally breaks away, he says, "We had a breakthrough with Subject Thirteen." He delves into formula mixtures, rattling off metrics and readings, his excitement turning frenzied. "It's only a matter of time—"

I press my finger over his mouth, silencing his manic spiel and talk of time. "Don't tell me," I say. "Show me."

He smiles and nips my fingertip, then hauls me out of the chair and into his arms. He passes the doorway leading to his lab and instead enters the bedroom.

"You're taking me the wrong way."

He halts at the base of our bed and drops me on top of the feather comforter. Peering down at me with hooded eyes, Alex reaches behind his head and tugs his shirt off, revealing the defined, leanly carved muscles of his chest and abdomen.

"Correction," he says, as he moves in to cover my body with his. "I'm taking you. Period."

As we conduct our own feverish chemistry experiment between the sheets, embracing all that is violent and needy and loving within us, we accept the choices that wove our fate together.

Alex chose to love his monster.

And I chose to stay in my Wonderland with my dark prince.

Thank you for reading *Malady*, lovely reader! I hope you enjoyed Blakely and Alex's dark journey to find the light in each other. Please consider leaving a review, even a short one, as it means so much to authors. Thank you!

If you're not yet ready for us to part, as am I, I'd like to take you further, dare you to go even darker. Flip the pages to meet one of London's colleagues, Sadie Bonds, in **With Visions of Red**, a thrilling, killer romance with a dark and shocking twist.

FREE BOOK OFFER

Special gift to Trisha Wolfe readers! Receive a FREE novelette featuring your favorite dark romance couple, London and Grayson, from the ***Darkly, Madly Duet*** .

We weren't born the day we took our first breath. We were born the moment we stole it.

~Grayson Peirce Sullivan, *Born, Darkly*

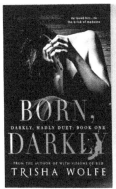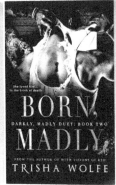

Want more London and Grayson from *Malady*? Meet Grayson Sullivan, AKA The Angel of Maine serial killer, and Dr. London Noble, the psychologist who falls for her patient, as they're drawn into a dark and twisted web. The ultimate cat and mouse game for dark romance lovers.

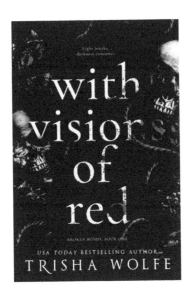

He knows her secrets. Her obsessions. The darkest, most deviant part of her soul. Plunged into a world of torture and suffering, pain and pleasure, Sadie Bonds and Colton Reed balance on the razor-sharp edge of two intersecting worlds threatening to swallow them as they hunt a serial killer.

Colton

I watch her.

Since her first visit to The Lair months ago, I've been watching. Just watching. And she watches, too.

I assumed she was a voyeur. Only here to feed some curiosity, or feast on the sight of flesh and violence. But the longer I watch, the more I see it in her jade eyes.

She's hungry.

How she even got through the front door, I don't know. Julian must have been feeling charitable that first night. Maybe thinking the same as me—that she was just wanting to settle some curiosity. But here she is again. It's her MO.

I round the bar, tapping Onyx on the shoulder to let her know I'm taking off. Then I duck under the bar top, the beat of the house music thumping in sync to my ramped heart rate.

She hasn't been back for a while. Maybe two weeks. And I'm like a hunter stalking my prey, needing to get a long, lustful gaze at my conquest. Although, truth be told, I have no intention of making a move on her. She's too perfect. I just want to marvel, to watch as she watches, taking in her labored breaths. Her fingers clamped tightly around her flute of champagne.

I lean my shoulder against the wall and fold my arms over my chest and black T-shirt, letting my gaze travel over the room until it locks on to her.

This is just one room in the club. The voyeur. Set up with a stage and plenty of space for the audience to roam and play while each scene is enacted for the members' enjoyment.

I've wondered before if she ever visits the other rooms. If she ever visits mine...if she plays...but I'm trusting my instincts on this one. That, and the fact Julian has confirmed he's never set her up with a Dom or Domme.

Okay, fine. I've asked about her. Even against my better judgment and Julian's unwelcome probing into my life.

All my thoughts cease as the scene on stage begins. The music dies down, and in the sudden, stark silence, a low and melodic beat starts. The dungeon master walks a blindfolded woman onto the stage and commences strapping her to a St. Andrew's cross.

It's a classic scene, one that the sub requests each week. She likes to be flogged while a Dom frees her from her daily monotony as a CEO of some company. Then she prefers her master to go down on her as she climaxes.

But it's the first time *she's* been witness to it. And I move a bit closer, needing a clear view of her face as she watches. My heated breath coasts past my lips, slow and measured, as I spy her vivid eyes trained on the scene. Her lips parted, black dress clinging to the curves of her slim body.

Her chest rises with her sudden and deep inhale. The V of her dress teases me, the creamy skin of her chest hidden beneath a scarf, the round swells of her breasts just below, inviting.

From the corner of my vision, I see the flogger make contact across the sub's tits, and my pants tighten painfully as my target's hand goes to her chest. She caresses her smooth skin beneath that infuriating scarf as if she's been struck.

I slide my tongue over my lips as she crosses her legs. I imagine her thighs pressing together tightly, putting needed pressure against her clit, her panties wet. *Fuck*. I reach down and adjust myself. This is getting ridiculous, how much I crave this stranger, but she's not like the others.

So many tempting beauties occupy this scene, and though I've played with my fair share, and it was satisfying on a carnal level, I've never been entranced the way I am when I watch her.

What would it feel like to tie her down and discover what she desires? For her to let me in and reveal her darkest fantasies? To extract her fears and inflict them on her, making her tremble, scream, *ache*. Then fall to my knees and gratify her as I worship my goddess.

The muffled cry from the stage cracks into my musings with the strike of the flogger, and I'm awoken from my trance, only to fall into my own form of torment.

I watch as my goddess becomes bold as the other members play around her. She snakes her hand up her parted thighs, under the hem of her dress. Her eyes shut against the scene as she touches herself.

Fucking hell. I'm going to come undone.

Yes, beauty. Rub that slick, swollen clit.

I reach down and run my palm over the rock-hard bulge pressing against my jeans. I feel the connection to her as she pushes her hem up enough for me to witness her sliding her panties aside, then I envision her trembling finger sliding into her warm flesh. Her eyes are clamped closed against the darkness, her breasts straining against the taut fabric, her nipples peaked.

I want to be there with her. Right there, when she comes. I'm tempted to yank my cock out this instant and beat the fucker off.

But my hand stills, my breathing catches in my throat, as a guy moves in front of my line of vision. Dammit. I'm already stepping closer to get around him when my feet stop. I watch as he lays his hand on her shoulder, then bends over to whisper in her ear.

My hands curl into fists.

If she welcomes his advance, I'm going to lose my shit. I won't be able to stand here and watch someone else give her what I know she needs. Fuck him. He hasn't watched her for months; he hasn't logged away countless hours discovering what she yearns for.

And he sure as shit doesn't know that she doesn't want to be touched. But I do—and I'm two seconds away from breaking his hand.

I keep watching, regardless. If she's ready to play, finally, I'll make sure she's safe. I'll watch over her, protect her.

She's shaking her head, trying to get away from him. She's rattled. He's not what she wants. She's here to watch, not play. She's not ready.

Relieved, I slowly back away. I'm pissed hot that he

interrupted our moment, but there will be another. There's always another. She's getting bolder.

And so am I.

Only when I glimpse the distress on her face, her panic mounting, I immediately stop.

The guy touches her again, this time on her waist. He's leaning over her, trying to persuade her to join him. He grips her around one thin wrist and forcefully pulls her against him.

That's breaking the rules, fucker.

I'm storming toward him before Onyx can alert the bouncer.

His hand slides around her stomach as she pushes away from him, fear marring her gorgeous face.

"She said *no*." Towering over the guy, I bring all of my six-foot self forward, a dominant shadow cast over him. I haven't touched him. Yet. But my fists are locked, every muscle corded tight.

The guy—who's wearing a dark-gray business suit —straightens his back to bring himself fully before me. "She wants it. She's just shy." He glances down at her. "Needs a little persuading."

Hot breaths saw in and out of my nose. "The lady wants to watch. No means *no*, asshole. In any establishment, but especially here." Hiking my thumb over my shoulder, I say, "I think you've played enough for tonight."

His eyes narrow, but he shrugs, deciding it's not

worth the consequences if he wants to take this matter further. He gives me a once over, sizing me up, before he walks around and leaves.

Releasing a strained breath, I let the adrenaline ebb, gaining my composure before I look down at her.

When I finally do, my muscles go lax. She's mortified. I can see it painted clearly all over her beautiful face, splashed with red, even in the darkness.

I kneel down, my whole body strung tight with the need to touch her. I've anticipated this moment—when we'd first look at one another; when I'd hear her voice —but I hate that it's like this. With fear in her deep-green eyes. At least, fear that I didn't put there.

"He's a douchebag," I say. "Are you okay?"

Her burgundy layers fall to conceal her face, and I want so badly to push them aside. It's a wig—I realized this before now. I've imagined what her real hair looks like; dark, to match her eyebrows. Soft, silky, long. I want to strip her of the fakeness and curl my fingers around a thick hank of her real hair. Pull her head back, look down into her eyes. I push the enticing thought away.

She nods a couple times, her movements jerky. "I'm fine. Just embarrassed, I guess." Lifting her chin, she fixes her penetrating gaze on me. All logic flees my brain. "But what did I expect? I mean, look at where I am. I overreacted, that's all."

Blinking hard, I break the hold she has over me,

searching for the right words. I need to please her in this moment, but god, I'm already so lost to her.

"You should expect members to behave appropriately, at the very least," I say. "You're not doing anything wrong by being here, watching. That's what this room is all about. He knows the rules." I nod my head toward the black wall, where submissives are lined up in knelt positions. "You're not on your knees. You're not asking to be dominated. There's always a bad apple, and it just looks like one found you."

Long eyelashes frame her widening eyes. She's staring right into the depths of me. "Don't blame the victim," she says, her voice throaty. "I know that by heart. You'd think I'd believe it by now."

I feel my brow furrow slightly. It's as if she's talking more to herself than me, but I tuck this interesting morsel of information away. "That's right. Now," I say, moving a fraction closer. "I'm technically off work. So I'd like to help you get back to enjoying yourself."

The slender column of her throat bobs on a swallow. "I'm not into…"

"Shh," I say. "I won't lay a hand on you. I won't touch you. And I can leave…if that makes you more comfortable." I pause, praying that my goddess doesn't send me away.

When she doesn't speak up immediately, I push on. "I only want to see that look in your eyes, that passion on your face—the one you wore just moments before that rude interruption."

I watch as her breathing quickens. The tremble of her red, red lips. "No touching?" she questions.

My pulse speeds. "Only if you ask. *Always,* only if you ask."

She continues to stare at me in guarded fascination, the seconds suspending us in our own sphere of heat and caution. When she gives a sure nod, I'm lit with fire.

As she swivels her stool to face the stage, I peer down at her, amazed at this stunning creature I've somehow discovered. I pull another stool up close behind her and take my seat.

Her shoulders tense as my thighs and body cage her in from behind. I can feel her body heat radiating off her, caressing me, beckoning me. Her fragrance of sweet-scented shampoo and body lotion fills my senses, tantalizing.

Slowly, carefully, I lower my head next to hers. As close to her as I can get without touching. With difficulty, I aim my attention toward the stage. The Dom is placing nipple clamps on the sub, her high-pitched moans piercing the charged air between us.

"Do you know why he connects the chain to her mouth gag?" My words slip past my lips in a whispered plea.

She remains silent, her gaze steady on the scene. A

slight shake of her head invites me to continue, and my dick swells.

"It heightens her desire. Her awareness." I breathe her in, a glutton, needing to satisfy my senses. "It also heightens her suffering, increasing his pleasure."

As the flogger makes contact against the sub's stomach, she jerks her head, pulling the chain taut. "He's punishing her for moving," I continue, "but that sharp spike of pain gives her so much pleasure, that she can't help but be disobedient. She needs the punishment almost as much as she needs the release, the gratification."

My gaze flicks lower as my goddess squeezes her thighs together. I bite down on my bottom lip, inducing a slight pain to keep my emotions in check, my head clear.

The need to slip my arms around her and hike up that damn dress…spread those legs wide…is almost unbearable. I grip my jeans near my knees, clenching the rough material, to keep my hands from roaming.

This—it's not nearly enough. But as the wisps of her hair caress my cheek, hinting at her trembling body, I revel in this profound moment my goddess is gifting me. To indulge in her—to enter into her sanctity. She's my temple and I'm her slave, willing to kneel before her on command.

And as she tentatively runs a finger along her thigh, drawing up the hem of her dress, sliding her hand between her thighs…god, the anguish is pure hell. A torment so divine, I nearly come undone.

I will beg for more.

I'm not ashamed to own it—to confess what I've been craving for months.

"Can you feel what she feels?" I ask, my voice husky with restrained want.

I watch her tongue slip out to wet her lips as she gazes at the scene, and I grit my teeth. The sub—now sated from her penance—throws her head back in bliss. The Dom hikes one of her legs over his shoulder as he kneels before her, devouring her, taking her into his mouth with unguarded vigor.

"She's stripped raw, laid bare," I whisper. "She's utterly vulnerable to him. Having submitted her whole being over to him, she's now free to indulge in the ecstasy which comes from that liberating relinquishing of control."

She shudders next to me, and my eyes follow the trail of her hand upward. Farther and farther—so painstakingly slow—until she's there. Her head lolls to the side, her eyes close, and we're lost together as she caresses herself through the thin barrier of her black panties.

"I wish I could have that," she admits, so low, and my whole body is piqued, awaiting her next admission.

"What do you need?" I ask, my fingers curled so tightly around my jeans they ache, could shred the fuckers. My dick is so hard, I swear, it's going to rip straight through my jeans.

"To be free," she whispers.

I squeeze my eyes closed against the severe quake that her softly spoken words elicit. "Slide your panties aside."

I'm just in control enough to open my eyes and witness her obeying my order. A primal need to throw her down and ravish her—right here; right now—barrels through me.

"Push inside. Deep. Until it aches." God, but she does. Holy hell, she spreads those sweet thighs and sinks her finger inside until I hear her desperate moan. "Fucking move your hips. Go deeper…"

A shrill moan resounds around us, and the spell is broken.

Her eyes fly open and she stares at the stage, to where the sub is coming with fierce and quivering pleasure as she pulls at her restraints.

"Relax," I say, restraining myself from touching her. "Let me be the one to take you there. Just like that. Let me—"

She sits forward. Pushes her dress back down her legs. "Shit. I need to go."

"Wait." I almost reach out for her, but I stop mid-air. My hand balls into a tight fist. "Don't run. This is what comes next. Let yourself experience it."

She shakes her head, shame creasing the tight

corners of her eyes. "It always pulls me under," she says. At my confused expression, she clarifies, "The darkness. It's always there…with the cries. I don't deserve the freedom you're offering. That's not why I'm here."

Then she's gone before I can demand to know more, my beautiful goddess vanishing as quickly as she appeared.

And, oh—I'm so tempted to give chase and beg her to welcome me into her darkness.

The desire to follow her thrums through me with vicious abandon.

I close my eyes, slip my hand into my pocket, and caress the rough cord of rope to drive away the coldness encasing me in my own dark, hollow space.

She will understand soon there's no reason to hide from me, no reason to be ashamed. I understand her; I appreciate her fear more than any other soul.

Soothed, I open my eyes. I won't be able to wait until she appears next in my world before I see her again.

ABOUT TRISHA WOLFE

From an early age, Trisha Wolfe dreamed up fictional worlds and characters and was accused of talking to herself. Today, she lives in South Carolina with her family and writes full time, using her fictional worlds as an excuse to continue talking to herself. Get updates on future releases at TrishaWolfe.com

Want to be the first to hear about new book releases, special promotions, and signing events for all Trisha Wolfe books? Sign up for Trisha Wolfe's VIP list at TrishaWolfe.com

Connect with Trisha Wolfe on social media on these platforms: Facebook | Instagram | TikTok

ACKNOWLEDGMENTS

Thank you to:

My amazingly talented critique partner and friend, P.T. Michelle, for reading so quickly, giving me much needed pep talks and advice, wonderful notes, and for your friendship.

My super human beta readers, who read on the fly and offer so much encouragement. Melissa & Michell (My M&M's), and Debbie for offering me so much helpful insight as always. All the girls in The Lair for reading the ARC and cheerleading. Your excitement keeps me going! I really can't express how much you girls mean to me—just know that I couldn't do this without you.

To all the authors out there, my kindred, who share and give shouts outs. You know who you are, and you are amazing.

To my family. My son, Blue, who is my inspiration, thank you for being you. I love you. To my husband, Daniel (my turtle), for your support and owning your title as "the husband" at every book event. To my personal assistant, my PA of freaking amazing, Meagan, who rescued me from the cliff and became my family. I have no idea what I'd do without you, and I hope to never find out.

There are many, oh, so many people who I have to thank, who have been right beside me during this journey, and who will continue to be there, but I know I can't thank everyone here, the list would go on and on. So just know that I love you dearly. You know who you are, and I wouldn't be here without your support. Thank you so much.

To my readers, you have no idea how much I value and love each and every one of you. If it wasn't for you, none of this would be possible. As cliché as that sounds, I mean it from the bottom of my black heart. I adore you, and hope to always publish books that make you feel.

Made in the USA
Monee, IL
20 June 2022

98283677R00184